NOBLE SECRETS

AN AETHER PSYCHICS NOVELLA

CECILIA DOMINIC

ABOUT NOBLE SECRETS

A dangerous man from her past.
A handsome duke in her present.
Secrets that threaten their future.

After tragedy hits and danger moves in, Pauline Danahue flees London, searching for sanctuary and a way to start over. A job at a small university provides the escape she needs. Keeping recalcitrant professor Edward Bailey on task after a shattered heart renders him broken and destroyed becomes her daily routine. But when the same vicious man from her past sets his malicious sights on Pauline, her safe haven comes crashing down.

Duke of Waltham, Christopher Bailey, never counted on the gentle commoner, Miss Danahue, to save his brother–and himself–from broken pasts and a lifetime of mistakes. But she does just that.

As their love blossoms, danger closes in, threatening Pauline and Christopher's lives. Together, they are forced to face their biggest fears, revealing secrets that could ruin them both.

1

———

D*epartment of Aetherics, Huntington University, 4 July 1862*

PAULINE LOOKED up from her newspaper. It was still early, and she'd been enjoying the summertime quiet, but the sound of men's voices ascending the stairs—presumably attached to her bosses—meant it was time to get back to work. She folded the paper and put it in her large reticule so no one would see her reading it. In spite of the university being a bastion of learning, it was frowned upon for the staff—well, female staff—to engage in intellectual pursuits.

She turned on the steam kettle and set up the tea tray, turning in time to see four men walk into the front hall of the department.

Dean Hartford led the charge. Pauline mentally ticked off what he would want - Earl Grey, extra strong. Two blueberry scones. No butter. Then the chairman, Harold Kluge, the same but with only one scone. Then the blond gentleman. He looked familiar, and Pauline's intuition said he would only want tea. The same for the fourth one, who—

The deep blue of his eyes and his tired smile made Pauline want to lead him to a chair, fluff his pillow, and put a nip of brandy in his tea. She shook her head. He resembled Edward Bailey, a young professor whose genius had allowed him to take a faculty position at an early age, but she'd never had that kind of response to the finicky academic, who liked his sugar cubes split.

"Pauline, tea in the conference room, please," the dean said. His normally booming voice was subdued, which only heightened the tension in the air.

Pauline fixed everyone's tea the way they wanted it that morning and arranged the pots for balance. She ignored the twinge in her shoulder when she hoisted the tray. That pain emerged at the most inconvenient times, and she shook off the memory of the large hand grabbing her by the upper arm and slamming her against the wall. That had been another girl in another life.

She paused in front of the closed conference room door and huffed. How did they expect her to carry the tray and open the door? She couldn't even knock with her elbow for fear of upsetting the very full teapot with the extra strong Earl Grey, and she dared not call for fear of annoying some faculty member in some office on the hall.

She would have to go back to her desk, offload some of the items, and come back. Before she turned, the door swung inward, and the blue-eyed young man took the tray from her so quickly she squeaked.

"Sorry," he mouthed.

"Quite all right."

"...able to work?" Chairman Kluge was saying. He shot an annoyed look at Pauline. "Please serve the tea without comment, Miss. This is a serious discussion. As I was saying,

Your Grace, we have a patent application underway for a new aether isolating device, and Professor Bailey is indispensable to the process. If we delay, I fear those snobs at Oxford will beat us to it."

Your Grace? Pauline looked at her savior with curiosity. He seemed young to be a duke, but then it all clicked into place.

Of course! Professor Bailey had an older brother, and he was the son of a late duke. As she was new in town, she still sorted through the tangle of titles and identities.

"I'm concerned as to his mental welfare," the duke said. "You know he's always been, well, Mother describes him as quirky. Different. Sensitive. He's had his first heartbreak, and it's going to keep him from being able to work efficiently. He is inclined to just stop what he's doing and stare off into space."

Pauline poured the tea and listened with interest. She liked Professor Bailey just fine but recognized he was an unusual sort, very much in his own head. Considering her experience had been with men who preferred not to think too much about what they were doing and to whom, she appreciated his intense focus on his work.

"I still don't understand how she could have thought he was you, Christopher," the blond young man said. He lounged with a languid air, and he raised his eyebrows when Pauline handed him his tea fixed exactly as he liked it. She mentally kicked herself—she should have remembered to make a show of asking, but she was distracted by his familiarity in calling the duke by his given name.

"Lucky guess," she whispered.

He grinned, and she looked away, her face heating. She knew his sort—he would be one to make a big show of attending to a woman's desires, making her think she meant something to him, and then leaving her cold in the morning. She rotated her shoulder against the pain that had become a stubborn needle at the top of the blade.

The duke didn't answer the question of how the professor had been mistaken for him. "The important thing is what to do with him now. He would have gotten his heart broken eventually, so it's good he got it over with."

"You make heartbreak sound like a disease," the dean said.

"Isn't it?" the blond man asked. "That's why I avoid it."

"Yes, Maestro, we're familiar with your romantic philosophies," Chairman Kluge snapped. "Let's get back to the matter at hand. How are we to keep Professor Bailey on track with developing the device?"

"It sounds like you need someone to watch him and ensure he's working, not mooning about," the dean mused. "A babysitter, as it were."

"It's a good thing he's a genius," Kluge muttered. "Maestro? Are you free this summer?"

"'Fraid not, old chap." The blond gentleman hoisted his teacup. "Got a full summer concert lineup."

"I wish I could help," the duke put in, "but I have an estate to run."

Pauline edged toward the door. She felt the tide of opinion shifting, and she certainly didn't want to get roped into watching the moody professor. She'd babysat enough men in her time, and the thought of attending to a finicky academic made her stomach fold in on itself and the needle of pain in her shoulder twist into a knife.

"Miss Danahue's duties are light at the moment with so many of the staff being away for the season," Chairman Kluge said. "She can help out."

Pauline stopped, her hand on the door handle, and said in her sweetest voice, "Of course I'm happy to, but are you sure you don't need me for other things?"

"No, that seems to be the best solution," the dean said. "You will watch Professor Bailey and ensure he finishes the aether isolating device development and patent application."

"I'd greatly appreciate it," the duke said. Pauline sensed his deep exhaustion.

She nodded and forced her jaw to relax as she smiled, hoping it looked genuine. "Of course, Your Grace."

WHEN CHRISTOPHER LEFT the Department of Aetherics, he paused and rubbed his eyes, which itched from lack of sleep. It had been a few long days. First there had been the cryptic telegram from Edward saying that everything had gone wrong and he wasn't coming back from the seaside because it would be too embarrassing. Then Christopher had gone to fetch him at the behest of their mother, and they'd arrived back so late that he had slept little before coming to the meeting at the University.

But if he were to be honest, guilt had kept him up during the brief time he'd had to sleep, poking his chest with its needle-sharp claws every time he tried to drift off.

"Are you all right?" Johann Bledsoe, a violinist and Edward's best friend, stood beside him. "I'd forgotten how intense those academics can be."

"Just tired." Christopher wondered how much Johann remembered of the party and the disastrous prank he had played on his own brother. "Do you need a ride back to the country?"

"Thanks, but I'm keeping a low profile with the family. Plus the first summer concert is this evening."

"Right." Christopher's mind couldn't keep up with the days since the first part of the week had distorted in carnival mirror fashion. "At least you have the option to lay low."

They walked toward the park that the university had designated for the use of steam vehicles. Christopher's driver sat with the steamcoach reading a book.

"Do you think Miss Danahue will be able to keep Edward in line?" Johann asked. "She seemed a clever sort, or at least resourceful."

Christopher didn't want to say what he'd thought of the young secretary. The beauty of her face and the haunted look in her dark eyes had been the first things to truly pierce his brain fog that morning. Part of him was glad she'd be watching Edward because it would give Christoper the excuse to watch her.

"I suppose we'll see," he said. They'd reached the lot. "Now if you'll excuse me, I'm going to Waltham Manor to try to set my mother's mind at ease."

"Right." Johann tipped his hat and walked toward town.

Christopher got into the coach and settled into the cushions. The vehicle rolled forward, the sound of gravel under the wheels smoothing to the hiss of the inlaid rails of the street. He wished he could as easily leave behind Johann's earlier question. Christopher knew how Lily Cavender had mistaken Edward for him, and the knowledge fed his guilt.

The chuffing of the steamcoach's engine and the fresh warm summer air coming through the windows lulled him into a fitful sleep, but all too soon he arrived at the manor.

The coachman opened the door, and Christopher alighted. Waltham Manor loomed over him, its dark stone echoing the sternness of the slate gray sky. A few drops splashed him as he dashed to the front door, and a rumble of thunder chased him inside.

"Did you get everything straightened out?"

Somehow his mother always knew when he would be home and waited for him in the front hallway. She leaned with both hands on her cane. The gloom from outside appeared to have seeped in, and the grand staircase stretched into the darkness of the upper landing. The family portraits' eyes glowed when lightning flashed.

Christopher rubbed the grit from his face and sneezed. The steamcoach's wheels kicked up less dust than a team of horses, but it had still been unwise to keep the windows open. He'd meant to close them once the vehicle left the cobblestones of town with their smooth inlaid tracks for steam-powered coaches such as his, but he'd been enjoying a dream of a pretty secretary.

"Christopher?"

He snapped out of his dreamy—or nightmarish—fog. "Yes, we agreed on someone to babysit Edward. Kluge won't even charge for it."

"When does a university administrator pass up an opportunity for money?"

Christopher chuckled. Although she was ill, the duchess maintained her sharp mind.

"Since he's concerned about a patent application Edward's been working on. They're trying to beat Oxford, whose aetherics department is going to submit something similar."

"And who will be watching Edward?" Her gray eyes lit with a flash from outside.

"A secretary. Pauline Danahue."

The duchess wrinkled her brow. "I don't know that name. She's not from the area, is she?"

Christopher saw where that conversational track was going, and irritation flared in his chest at the thought of going back and making different arrangements. "It doesn't matter. She's the department secretary, and she's competent."

"You know I'm concerned about your brother and his fragile emotional state." This time the flash of lightning emphasized the thinness of the skin around her eyes.

"Don't worry about it, Mother. I'll check in on Miss Danahue. You need to rest."

He took her elbow with a gentle but firm hand and settled her in the parlor. He ignored the musty smell that lingered no matter how often they opened the windows. The doctors had all agreed—the duchess would likely not make it to Christmas, although Christopher knew she was stubborn enough to live longer just to prove them all wrong.

"Now if only I could get you settled," she said as she reclined. He fluffed the pillow behind her and covered her with a blanket. In spite of the warmth of the house, her touch chilled him as though all the heat in her body was going to her middle, where cancer ate at her.

"Don't worry about me. I'll marry when the time is right."

"This place needs a woman's touch, Christopher. And the townhouse—it's shameful how you and Edward have turned it into a bachelor's haven." The corners of her mouth tightened, the only sign she ever gave that she felt the gnawing on her insides to the point she couldn't ignore the pain.

Christopher rang the little bell that stood on the table beside her.

A maid carrying a tray entered, and Christopher mixed a few drops of laudanum into his mother's tea. He handed it to her and supported her as she drank.

"You'll not distract me from this conversation," she said, but her words slurred as she continued to speak. "I'm going to hold a ball a week from tomorrow, and I'll invite all the eligible young ladies. Except Lily Cavender, of course. Deceitful twit." Her eyelids fluttered, and she murmured, "A grand ball. Surely you will find someone who suits you. You're being stubborn like your father..." Her breathing evened, and Christopher smoothed the iron gray hair back from her face.

"And you," he said. He kissed her forehead and gave the laudanum bottle back to the maid. He followed the girl into the chief housekeeper's small office.

"Is she really serious about this ball idea?" he asked Mrs. Selby, who had run the household since he had been a child.

The older woman nodded and gestured to the lists on her desk. "I'm afraid so, Your Grace."

Christopher sighed. "You and I both know she's not well enough. Has Doctor Phillips been consulted?"

"She was having a good morning when he came."

"Of course she was. Or she was putting on a good show."

Mrs. Selby lifted her shoulders in a shrug of surrender, and she looked down, but the wetness in her eyes was apparent. "I don't have the heart to refuse her anything right now, Your Grace."

The irritation flared again—both at the housekeeper for humoring his mother's wishes to push him into a marriage he didn't desire and at the doctor for allowing the duchess to shorten her already waning days with the effort.

"Just keep it reasonably sized," he snapped, then added to soften his words, "for her health. She'll want to greet everyone personally."

The housekeeper nodded. "I know you're worried about her. We all are. I'll do what I can."

Christopher knew his mother well enough by now. She'd get her way with the ball, but he didn't have to bow to her will with a wife. Edward's experience had shown him what those noble girls were made of—deception and cunning—and he wanted none of it.

Edward has his work at the university. Why can't I be left alone to manage the estate as I see fit?

"Will you be eating dinner here?" Mrs. Selby asked. "I can tell Cook if you are."

"No, I just needed to check on Mother and reassure her. Edward is back at the townhouse, so I'll go back there and make sure he eats. Tonight is also the first summer concert."

He took the smaller steamcart from the stable and waved off the driver. "I need the time to think, and driving will help," he said.

"Yes, sir. Be careful—the roads are muddy."

"Will do."

He'd intended to enjoy the fresh-washed look of the trees and shrubbery on the roadside, but his thoughts echoed the rhythm of the engine.

What do I want in a wife? Do I even want one right now? Women are a bloody lot of trouble for the effort you have to put into them. What would happen if I kept driving, down through London and to the coast?

But the thought of another long day on the road made the idea of escape a fleeting one.

Department of Aetherics, Huntington University, 4 July 1862

ALTHOUGH PAULINE KNEW she was the best person to help Professor Bailey, she resisted the idea. She batted it back and forth in her brain like a cat with a ball of yarn. Yes, she could determine what he needed and use the knowledge to keep him on course with the patent. No, she didn't want to have to use her extra keen intuition, at least right now. It brought back memories of her own mother, who would do the same for her clients.

Pauline remembered as many men coming to her for comfort after heartbreak or business disappointments as for satisfaction of carnal desires. And that was what made her shudder about the role she was to play—her mother's talent had been what killed her in the end, and her death had come at the hands of a jealous man. Once she'd lost her mother's protection, Pauline had been vulnerable, her position as a maid to the prostitutes and a dancer to entertain the guests while they waited suddenly tenuous. One night one of the clients had gotten rough with her when she'd rebuffed his advances, slamming her into a door frame and injuring her shoulder. The brothel owner had done nothing, and Pauline had known it was only a matter of time before the madame made her join the girls who entertained the men behind closed doors rather than in the parlor... Or sell her to the murderer.

That was why she had run away.

She nodded to Chairman Kluge as he exited his office at the end of the day.

"Aren't you leaving as well?" He checked his watch. "It's after five o'clock."

"Oh, so it is."

He hovered while she gathered her things and locked up. She made sure the newspaper stayed safely tucked out of sight. Keeping abreast of the news in London—and the murders committed there—was part of her survival, and she didn't want her main source of information to be confiscated because women were too delicate to read about such horrible things.

"May I walk you out?" he asked.

If Pauline hadn't possessed her talent, she would have thought he wanted to start an affair with her. He was happily married as far as she knew—she'd chosen that department to work in for that reason and because the aetherists seemed more inclined to be in their head than to notice women. No, she sensed he wanted reassurance that she was up to the task of watching Professor Bailey.

She followed him out and waited for him to speak. She didn't have to wait long.

"Professor Bailey will be returning tomorrow," he said. "I don't know what time, so can you be early?"

"Yes," she said. She didn't have anywhere else to be, and she certainly didn't plan to be out late that evening.

"You haven't interacted with him much yet, but you've probably discerned he's different," Kluge warned. "Not as charming as many young men, but at least you'll know where you stand with him."

"I can handle that," she said. "I prefer straightforwardness to deceit."

"Good. He does, too. He still hasn't forgiven me for something he thinks I exaggerated when I hired him."

She wanted to ask what, but she knew he would volunteer the information if he wanted her to know.

They walked into the soft summer air. She took a deep breath to clear her nose of the old paper and chemical smells of the department and caught a whiff of something floral.

"Are you all right walking to your home alone?" he asked. Now he didn't want anyone to see them together and assume the worst.

"Yes, thank you. It's a lovely evening, and it will be bright for a while, so I'll take my time."

He tipped his hat. "See you on the morrow, then."

She turned toward the poorer part of town where her boarding house was. She kept her extra sense alert for anyone wanting to do her harm and had just walked off campus when she felt something. It crept through the layers of scent on the breeze like the slimy grasping tendril of a poisonous plant. She paused and pretended to check her watch while trying to determine the direction from which it came. Her hands trembled at the sensation's familiarity. The man was behind her, so she turned into a nearby pub where the university staff liked to eat. She'd wait him out. Or she could slip away with the crowds after dinner —those headed to the summer concert.

"Can I help you, Miss?" The tavern keeper greeted her with a quizzical look.

Pauline cursed to herself. Of course she couldn't stay here. This wasn't the city, where she'd been known in the pubs to fetch things for the prostitutes who entertained their marks in the taverns along Flannery Street. A woman being in a public house would draw attention, and that was the last thing she wanted. Someone outside sought her, but she was sure he hadn't spotted her. She couldn't stay here, but she didn't want to leave, either.

"She's with us."

The deep voice startled Pauline, and she turned to see the sky blue eyes of Christopher Bailey looking at her. "Miss Danahue, I'm so glad you could meet us here. I believe you know my brother Edward?"

~

EDWARD'S DOCILITY in leaving the house for dinner worried Christopher. His younger brother seemed half-there and merely stared into space like an imbecile, not a professor with a formidable intellect. Seeing Miss Danahue gave Christopher a welcome distraction from what would have been a dull meal.

Plus, she intrigued him.

She looked uncomfortable, but he sensed that she was acting the part, rather than actually feeling that way. Most polite young ladies would be skittish in an atmosphere where some men sang loudly, others argued, and still others played dice or cards. But not her. Christopher's notice grew into curiosity.

After he told the barkeep she was with them, the man's beard spread into a smile. "You've got an interesting way of entertaining the young ladies, Your Grace."

"This is Miss Pauline Danahue," Christopher said. "She's helping me with a project."

Andrew showed them to a small round table in a relatively quiet corner. Edward flinched whenever the noise got too loud or close, but he didn't show much other reaction. Christopher ordered for him and turned to Miss Danahue.

"What would you like?" he asked. He scanned the menu for food that a young lady of breeding would be comfortable eating.

"Fish and chips, please," she said.

He couldn't help a delighted grin. "I've never seen a young lady who liked pub food. Most turn their noses up at it unless they're at a carnival."

She shrugged, but an odd emotion flickered over her face. She looked like she'd been caught at something. "I thought they looked like something I'd had once."

"Then you must try them with the malt vinegar. It really enhances the flavor."

"Thank you," she said. "For allowing me to join you. I don't know what I was thinking, coming in here."

He suspected she was lying, but she had looked rather perplexed when he'd seen her. His mother's question about her origins came to mind.

"Where are you from?" he asked.

"The city." She turned to Edward, who sat with his hands folded on the table in front of him. "Professor Bailey, I'm happy to see you again. I'm Pauline Danahue."

"You didn't think he'd recognize you?" Christopher asked. "How long have you been at the department?"

"Just a couple of weeks, and we met only briefly."

"He must have just gone to the seaside, then."

At the mention of his trip, Edward blinked and said, "Right, the sea." He looked around. "Where am I?"

"At Marlay's," Christopher told him. "You agreed to come out to dinner, remember?"

Edward looked like a man waking from a bad dream. "Oh, so then it wasn't real. I was afraid that would happen with the aether—that it would bend time around it like light and mix me up."

The image of the old duchess in her final illness flashed

through Christopher's mind. He had had enough with people denying reality to focus on silly things. He shoved his half-filled pint glass at Edward. "No, I'm afraid your trip and everything else truly transpired. Have some beer."

Edward shook his head and returned to studying his hands. Christopher cursed under his breath. He should have been gentler, but he couldn't handle everything with his mother alone. That he'd aimed Lily Cavender at Edward to get her out of his own hair only made Christopher's anger at himself flare up.

"Let me try." Miss Danahue's cool voice cut through his frustration. "Professor? Tell me about the aether."

Edward looked at her and shook his head. "You don't know? It's the substance light travels through. It's in the theoretical stage right now, equations and such. No one's ever seen it, but the mathematics support it." He gave her a thorough explanation that lasted until the food came. Then Edward stopped talking only long enough to take bites and chew as he demonstrated with chips what they thought about light and how it traveled.

Christopher had heard it all before and only understood half of it, but Miss Danahue surprised him again, this time by her apparent interest in what Edward was saying. It also gave him a chance to get his own thoughts and emotions under control, and he shoved the pint glass away. He couldn't afford to become fuzzy-headed with alcohol, although this pub catered to academic tastes—beer uninspiring enough to not get in the way of mental processing.

Seeing Miss Danahue handle Edward, asking just enough questions to keep him grounded in the reality of his work, his one true love, relieved some of Christopher's anxiety. She'd be up to the task, then. Even after Edward finished and turned to give his full attention to his food, he had more color in his face, and the dreamy look had cleared from his eyes.

"Thank you," Christopher mouthed.

She smiled, and warmth replaced the tension around his heart, especially when she leaned closer. "It was no problem," she murmured. "I was genuinely interested."

"That's why you're so good at your job," he said.

Her cheeks turned a lovely shade of rose, and she looked away. "I try. Academics are people like everyone else."

"And what about the nobility?" he couldn't resist teasing.

"They are, especially."

It felt intimate, their words flowing beneath the chatter and clatter of the pub. A few salt crystals flaked her lips, and he squashed the impulse to kiss them off. He barely knew her, after all, but he couldn't deny his admiration. She seemed so different from the society misses his mother kept throwing at him. They only saw him as a stepping stone to their ambitions of becoming the next Duchess of Waltham. Miss Danahue seemed to see people as they were.

He decided he would have to stop in and check on Edward's progress. Just to keep his mother and the university administration happy, of course.

PAULINE WAS SO CAUGHT up in the duke's stunning blue eyes she almost missed it when *he* came into the pub. She leaned back so her face was partially obscured by a pillar and glanced around while pretending to think about her next response.

Someone emanated that feeling of black, slimy vines grasping for her, but the pub was too crowded and the light inside too dim for her to make out individual faces. She clenched her fists under the table while maintaining a look of interest in what the duke was saying. He asked a question, and she nodded, but her mind struggled not to fall into the past, when she had first felt that horrible sensation of a monster looking for her.

If only her mother's murderer hadn't been wearing a mask. He had been someone important, and the madam had humored his desire to keep his identity obscured. He had visited her for months, and rumors swirled around him, some that he was the crown prince himself. But he paid well and even brought some notoriety to the brothel, so those in charge didn't question him. Pauline had always avoided him because she sensed his needs were darker than the others', and her mother always looked especially drained after his visits. When he'd left one morning, they found her mother dead. Pauline knew he had killed her.

The duke stood. Pauline snapped back to the present and allowed him to help her rise. She followed him out, keeping her head ducked and her profile low. When they emerged, the sun hovered over the horizon—had they been there that long?—and music floated through the air.

"I'll drop Edward at the townhouse, and then we can go on to the concert for a while before I walk you home."

Is that what she'd nodded yes to? Pauline wanted to hide, but she forced herself to consider the options. If the man who hunted her was in the pub—and she sensed he hadn't emerged—then slipping into the crowd would keep her safe. Plus having the protection of the duke might help her in the future.

The duke held out an elbow, and she took it. Her fingers involuntarily wrapped around his bicep. His steel-hard bicep. She glanced up to see if he'd noticed her little squeeze, and he grinned down at her. The anxiety in her stomach uncurled under his gaze and stretched into something unfamiliar and warm.

They dropped Edward at the duke's townhouse and walked toward the town square. The orchestra was in intermission, so the ocean-like roar of the crowd enveloped them. The farther away they got from the pub, the more Pauline relaxed. Or rather, the anxiety of being hunted was replaced by a different sort of tension, that of wanting to see where this attraction to the duke went but knowing that anything formal between them was impossible. She was only the daughter of a prostitute, after all. She didn't even know who her father was.

"I'm afraid I must return your hand to you," he said. Was that regret in his tone? "It was stupid of me to take it, but you looked like you'd run if I didn't. People will talk, and I don't want them to assume anything about my intentions toward you."

His words brought an unexpected sting to her chest, and she released his arm. Although she'd just been thinking something similar, she had to keep her shoulders from curling forward in a posture of defeat.

"Perhaps I should return to my lodgings," she said and regretted it. She sounded like a pouting debutante.

"Don't be ridiculous. Stay and enjoy the music. With me. I'll introduce you to the principal violinist, Johann Bledsoe. He's quite a character and is Edward's best friend, so he may be a good resource for you. He was at the meeting."

"I remember, but we've not been formally introduced." She couldn't help but return his smile, and she noticed how he already had the beginnings of laugh lines at the corners of his eyes. They reminded her of the responsibilities he must have, especially since the death of his father the year before. She'd overheard two of the other secretaries talking about it—and how handsome he was—after she started.

The duke nodded to people as they passed, and Pauline felt their curiosity brush over her. Now the crowd's murmuring followed her, waves turned toward her, and she struggled not to get caught in their desire to know what the duke was doing with her, how he felt about her, even though she found the same need growing in her own mind.

He led her to the refreshment area behind the stage, where orchestra members took their break with white wine and chilled punch. Pauline spotted the blond gentleman who had accompanied the duke to the department that morning. He held his violin in one hand and a glass of punch in the other as he chatted with another violinist.

"Is that him?" she asked.

"Ah, right. Johann!"

Bledsoe excused himself from the conversation and came toward them.

"Christopher, I'm glad you made it out. And with Miss Danahue?" He turned his charming smile on Pauline and bowed over her hand.

"Right. She accompanied me to dinner with Edward. She has a way with him, it seems."

"I can see why." His gaze was forward enough to make Pauline's cheeks heat.

She looked away. "It's not difficult," she said. "He loves his work."

"And that's the way to his heart," Bledsoe agreed. "I'm glad you two made it. Would you like some punch?"

"No, thank you," Pauline said. The atmosphere of the crowd had changed, and now the black, slimy sensation floated through it like a seaweed vine. "I'm afraid the heat is over-coming me. I should go."

"You do look pale," the duke said. "I'll pay a cab to take you to your lodgings."

Of course he wouldn't want to walk her to the cheap boarding house in the part of town that was more pitiful than seedy. Or was there a difference? She didn't argue. Rather, she allowed herself to be bundled into a cab.

Each clop of the horses' hooves echoed her thoughts —*stupid, stupid, stupid.* The duke had only been caught up in the moment when he had invited her to attend the summer concert with him. Or maybe he'd tried to repay her in some way for her kindness to his brother.

Either way, she would maintain a cool, professional distance from him. Girls like her didn't deserve attention from men like him.

PAULINE WAS STILL ARGUING with her thoughts when she opened the door to her boarding house. The thin piece of rope that held her key matched the atmosphere of the place—frayed, worn, and dingy—but it was all she could afford on her secretary's salary. It seemed a world away from the summer concert, and a memory pushed in of herself holding some sort of brightly-colored frozen treat while listening to music on a summer day. A sense of lost belonging made her blink back tears. She'd always felt out of place, and these hints of an early childhood past only frustrated her.

The sound of conversation came from the dining room, and she paused. Did she want to slip by and go up to her room, where she could sit on her bed and wallow in her thoughts? Or would she prefer the company of women of her station and their frivolous concerns?

A needle of homesickness pricked her heart. There had been a camaraderie of sorts among the whores at the brothel she'd been raised in. Sure, they competed for the richest or handsomest clients—that was part of the fun for the men going to the place—but when they were alone, they traded beauty tips and comforted each other.

Pauline wasn't ready to be alone, so she turned into the dining room. Some of the other women were maids who worked part-time in some of the noble families' townhouses. Since they only filled in as needed, they didn't live at their employers' houses. Only Sally, one of the maids, and Mrs.

Culvert, the owner of the boarding house, sat in the dining room, but their cackling made as much noise as if the room had been full.

Sally raised a cup of tea to Pauline when she entered. Pauline guessed her landlady added the "Mrs." as a sign of respectability since there was no evidence of there ever having been a Mr. Culvert.

"Have you heard the big news?" Sally asked.

"Where's yer head, Sally?" Mrs. Culvert grinned at Pauline with her three teeth. "Tea, dear? Theadora brought some biscuits from her place. Her mistress said they were stale but good enough for the likes of us. Have you eaten?"

"Thank you," Pauline said, not sure in what order to answer the questions. "And I've had supper."

Pauline helped herself to the weak brew that passed for tea. She knew Mrs. Culvert reused the leaves, but her mouth was dry from the salty dinner.

"What's the news?" she asked Sally once she'd served herself and sat.

"The old duchess is looking for a wife for her oldest son and is holding a ball a week from tomorrow. Rumor has it that she's invited all the eligible young ladies in the county."

"Oh." *Stupid, stupid, stupid.* "Will you be serving?"

"Aye, if I'm lucky. I'm hoping old Selby will remember me from the garden party at Easter."

Of course Pauline had no idea what garden party Sally referred to. She'd only arrived in June. At Easter her mother had still been alive, but Pauline had been planning her exit. The Madame had been looking at her like a prize breeder, and only her mother's influence had kept her from being put in a stall to be poked like the others. She'd chosen Huntington Village because it was small in size yet had a constant influx and exit of people due to the university.

Obviously she hadn't gone far enough, and she needed to

move on away from the murderer, but as far as she knew, he hadn't spotted her. If she could stay unnoticed, perhaps he would leave. She only sensed he sought her, not that he'd found her. Plus, she'd committed to helping Professor Bailey, no matter what his handsome brother did or said to confuse her.

A sharp pain in her arm brought Pauline out of her thoughts. The others looked at her like she'd missed a question.

"I'm sorry," she said. "Long day."

"I asked if you were reading your future in your tea leaves," Sally said. "If you were, it don't look like a good one."

"I guess you never know," Pauline replied. "And right now, no, it doesn't."

Sally stood. "Well, I'm off to bed. Helping at market in the morning."

Pauline and Mrs. Culvert said goodnight, and Sally left. Pauline stood as well, but Mrs. Culvert made a slashing motion with one hand.

"Not yet, missy. Sit yerself down. I need to have a word with ye."

Pauline sank onto the bench, her heart pounding. "Is there a problem?" she asked with her best imitation of the brothel mistress addressing rowdy patrons.

"Don't pull those airs with me. You told me you were from the country, but I knew I heard city in your accent."

Pauline stiffened against the sensation of an entire bowl of iced punch being poured down the back of her dress, and she placed her hands under the table so Mrs. Culvert wouldn't see the chillbumps that rose with her panic.

"What do you mean?" Pauline asked.

"Someone dropped this off." Mrs. Culvert pulled an already dirty piece of paper from her apron pocket and slid it across the table.

Pauline unfolded it. There was a crudely drawn picture that somewhat resembled her along with the words, *Wanted: runaway indentured servant. Reward - 100 pounds. Please remit information to...* And there was an address in the fashionable part of town.

"It's not me," Pauline said. "I've never been to America or any of the colonies." She fully intended to go someday, which was why she saved her money.

"I didn't think so. I'm not an idiot." Mrs. Culvert snatched the paper back. "But there's someone looking who wants to find you. Badly."

Pauline searched the older woman's face for any pity or kindness. Surely she'd had a hard enough life herself to have sympathy for a young woman trapped in unfortunate circumstances. But no, the gleam in Mrs. Culvert's eyes was that of greed. She also exuded the need to take revenge on any pretty young thing who might try to better herself.

"What do you want?" Pauline asked, hoping for something reasonable but not counting on it.

"It seems that an extra shilling a week would be good protection for ye." She tapped one claw-like nail on the paper.

Panic squeezed Pauline's heart. Four extra shillings a month? With what she already paid, that would trap her in this town for years.

"I don't know if I can afford that," she said. "What about sixpence extra per week?"

"I don't know if that's worth it." Mrs. Culvert imitated her. "You have until tomorrow morning to decide. Oh, and if you leave, I'm telling this 'ere gentleman who you are, and I'll find out where you go. I have my ways."

A shadow flashed over her face, and Pauline drew back. Now she knew how Mrs. Culvert had obscured her internal ugly side—she was a hex witch. The girls at the brothel had visited one occasionally for contraceptives and spells against disease. Pauline suspected the woman had been talented with herbs, and she'd only emanated benign intentions. Mrs. Culvert, on the other hand, took revenge for her own insecurities, and Pauline guessed that Mr. Culvert, if he'd existed, had paid dearly for an indiscretion. If the woman was that powerful, she would be able to track Pauline and send the evil intentioned man after her.

"It appears I have no choice, then."

Mrs. Culvert patted her hand, the shadow gone. "Good night, then, dearie."

Pauline fled to her room. It was stuffy, so she opened the window, grateful she was three floors up where the worst of the street smells wouldn't reach her. The sounds of the summer concert floated through the window, and she found herself drawn to it. She closed her eyes and imagined the duke leading her through the crowd by her hand and tucking her against his side as he introduced her to his peers, handing her a cup of punch while they chatted with the musicians.

With a shake of her head, she opened her eyes, and Mrs. Culvert's words floated into her head—*stale but good enough for the likes of us.*

"Because we're not good enough for the fresh biscuits or the good men," she muttered. She cleaned up and lay on her narrow, hard bed. She tried to sleep, but her mind stayed busy recalculating how long it would be until she could flee England.

3

H *untington Park, 4 July 1862*

CHRISTOPHER WATCHED the cab roll away, and even after it disappeared, he listened until the clop of the hooves faded into the percussion of the orchestra. He wasn't sure who he was angrier at—himself for offending Miss Danahue, for he had no doubt he had, or at Johann Bledsoe for doing what he always did—turning his infamous charm toward the prettiest woman in proximity. Miss Danahue was beautiful enough she'd attract plenty of the wrong kind of attention, but she didn't need it from a self-confirmed rake like Bledsoe.

Christopher shook his head and wondered for the hundredth time how Johann and Edward had become such good friends.

In friendship as in love, some things simply can't be explained.

He turned back toward the square but decided after a few steps to pass through and go to the townhouse. It was getting dark, and the roads between town and the manor were not well-lit. It wouldn't take much to stop a carriage or steamcart, and there had been rumors of thieves in the countryside. His exhaustion caught up with him, and he hid a yawn and detoured around the square so he wouldn't have to face any motivated mamas who might want to put their daughter in his sight before the ball.

Footsteps followed him from the square, and he put a hand to his waist before remembering he'd left his firearm at the townhouse. He cursed under his breath and sped up his steps. The ones following him stayed a certain distance behind him. Finally when he reached the townhouse and had a hand on the front door handle, he turned to see a man ascend the stairs of the one next to his. He relaxed and waved.

"Sorry, didn't mean to frighten you," the man said with some sort of accent. "That's why I didn't follow more closely."

The gloom kept Christopher from making out the details of the man's features—only a thin face, long nose, and a mop of dark wavy hair.

"That's all right. Can't be too careful nowadays."

"Too right. Well, good night." He unlocked the door and stepped inside.

The townhouse's butler, Horace, opened the door for Christopher.

"Good evening, Your Grace."

Christopher appreciated Horace's inability to be surprised. Unfortunately that characteristic came with a distinct lack of curiosity for matters outside the household.

Still, Christopher asked, "Do you know anything about our neighbor? I didn't realize the residence had been bought or rented. Last I heard, it was still being renovated."

"I have heard he is of the peerage, but he keeps his own company, and not much is known about him."

All right, that was more than Christopher expected. Still, he pressed, "And does he have a wife? Family?"

"None that I know of, Sir. Would you like me to have a bath drawn for you?"

"Yes, please." He recognized he was less than fresh from his traveling about, especially after a walk through the still air of the evening. "Is Edward already in bed?"

"Yes, sir."

"Good. Please be sure we're both up by seven tomorrow morning. He has a big day at the university."

PAULINE WAITED until she got to the university before making tea for herself so she could avoid both Mrs. Culvert and her awful brew.

There was no time for the newspaper today, for when she walked into the department, she found the Duke of Waltham standing in front of her desk. She found herself irrationally angry with him. How dare he give her the mixed signals of allowing her his arm and then taking it away before anyone could see them? She acknowledged her irrationality, but she couldn't direct her anger toward the true object of her ire—the man who stalked her.

"Edward is in his office," he said. "Your conversation with him last night did wonders, so he should hopefully not require too much watching today. Thank you."

"You're welcome." She shoved her reticule—now lighter by a shilling thanks to Mrs. Culvert—under her desk. She hadn't even been able to afford a tuppence for the paper that morning.

Not that she would have been able to read it. Her mental math had kept her awake late into the night beyond the end of the concert, and she had a wicked headache. Plus, she was hungry, and all she'd eaten were two of Lady Smythe's stale biscuits. She had more in her reticule but couldn't stomach the thought of them. There was no point in chipping a tooth she couldn't afford to have fixed.

"Is something wrong?" he asked.

Why is he still here?

"Nothing that's any of your concern," she said. She started the gas burner and put a kettle on. *The witch can't even make proper tea.*

"Bubble, bubble, toil and trouble," she muttered.

"You know Shakespeare?" he asked.

She bit back her retort, that she wasn't stupid. The brothel had a small library, and her mother had taught her to read.

Contrary to what people will tell you, the right kind of man likes a woman who can think. To think and converse on the topics of the day, you need to read, her mother had often said.

She'd never told Pauline whether she was preparing her to follow in her footsteps or if she had a more respectable future in mind for her daughter than brothel maid and dancer. Pauline sensed it was the latter, but her mother couldn't say anything since the brothel owners had supported them, likely thinking Pauline was an investment and putting her to work at mundane tasks as she could walk and carry things.

As much good as all that had done her.

"I like Shakespeare," she said, trying not to snap. "He wrote great plays about people both ordinary and noble."

She told her heart not to flip like it did when he smiled.

"Oh, that reminds me." He pulled something bundled in a handkerchief out of his pocket. "I'm sorry if it got squashed. Our cook makes incredible scones, and she calls these her Noble Scones." And then, before she could warm to the idea of him doing something randomly sweet for her, he added, "It's to say thanks for what you're doing for Edward."

She opened the cloth. The heavenly smells of butter, lemon,

and strawberries wafted up to her nose and swamped her bitter thoughts. Her stomach growled. "Thank you."

"You're welcome. You like it?"

She pinched off a corner and closed her eyes in bliss at how it almost melted on her tongue, the perfect combination of sweet and tart. She nodded.

"Good. I'll leave you to Edward, then."

Her mouth was too full of buttery goodness to say goodbye, but she waved and watched until he disappeared into the corridor leading to the stairs. She finished the scone, shook the crumbs out of the duke's handkerchief into her hand, and licked them off her palm. She would wash the square of cloth and return it.

Or give it to the professor. There's no guarantee I'll see the duke again. I should have asked him for payment when I had the chance.

The kettle whistled, and she made tea. She closed her eyes and did something she could only describe as listening. Yes, Professor Bailey would like tea, too. She fixed a small pot for him and one for herself and left hers to steep at her desk while she brought his to him. It was still early, and none of the other faculty were in yet, so she made hers extra strong, hoping it would soothe her head.

Christopher reached the head of the stairwell and stopped. He'd meant to ask Miss Danahue if she would like a little extra stipend. She was new to the university, and he suspected Chairman Kluge and Dean Hartford would take advantage of her naiveté. She might not know that watching over quirky professors wasn't part of her duties. From their discussions, he suspected she had at least some sense, but she might not have the courage to ask.

Or wouldn't she? He'd be the gentleman and not make her. With that decided, he turned back.

When he reached the end of the corridor and peeked around the doorjamb to ensure she was there alone, he saw her shake the crumbs from the scone into her hand and lick them off her palm. The sight of her small pink tongue brushing her hand nearly doubled him over with a stab of desire through his groin, and he had to lean against the wall. Thoughts flooded his mind.

I wonder what else she can do with that tongue. And hand. And...

He shook his head. The motion had been distinctly unlady-like, and he wondered what made her drop her usual composure to do such a thing when she could have been interrupted at any moment. His mind cataloged the gesture as something none of the young women of his acquaintance would do.

His mother's question floated back into his mind. What did he know about Miss Danahue? Her accent said she was from the city, but he wasn't sure of anything beyond that.

Well, aside of the fact that she was intelligent and apparently very good at handling his brother's quirks.

And she'd ended up in a pub the night before, something no upper- or middle-class woman would have done.

Whatever her background was, he felt odd standing there and watching her, so he turned back to the stairs and hoped he wouldn't run into anyone with the evidence of his reaction to her tongue-work tenting his trousers like a schoolboy's hard-on.

Well, I'm in a school. And she's an attractive female.

And he hadn't reacted like that to a woman since he'd been in his first awkward spurt of manhood. His father had brought him to Madame Reece's for the kind of education he wouldn't get at Eton, at least not experientially.

That reminded him, he hadn't visited Lucy in several months. She took care of his physical needs, but he found himself not interested in that kind of visit. On the other hand, Madame Reece had connections in London. If he wanted to make inquiries into Miss Danahue's past, she may best know how to do that and keep it discreet.

He *could* go through proper channels... But then his mother would find out, and he didn't want to worry her in her frail state. He was only curious, concerned for his brother's well-being in case Edward took an interest in the secretary.

Wasn't he?

PAULINE BROUGHT the tea into Professor Bailey's office. Like many at the university, it had a single set of windows, in front of which he'd set up his desk. The room was still littered with crates, some unopened, some opened and half-unpacked. The professor knelt in front of one of them and dug through the straw.

"It's in here somewhere," he muttered.

"Knock knock," she said and hoped her smile was of the convincing sort, not the *please don't do anything* odd type.

He looked up. "Oh, Miss Danahue." He frowned. "What are you doing here?"

She stifled a sigh, and a piece of sugar crunched between her molars, signaling her jaw's desire to clench. She forced it to relax—no sense in making her headache worse. Obviously Professor Bailey hadn't been informed of her assistance.

"I brought you some tea."

He frowned. With his facial muscles tight, he resembled his older brother. Pauline wondered just how young the professor was. His face still had the roundness of boyish youth, although his recent heartbreak was evident in the shadows under his eyes.

"What for? I've had breakfast."

"Tea helps you think," she suggested. She shrugged such that the cup rattled on its saucer and hoped he'd take the hint that she'd like to put the tray down somewhere.

He only continued to look at—no, through—her. She stepped back.

He rose, walked to the desk, and sat behind it, his fingers steepled in front of him.

"May I put this tray somewhere?" she asked finally. Her shoulder was giving her warnings that it wanted to give out, and she feared she'd drop the tea service.

He gestured to a stack of crates, and she placed the tray atop them, careful to ensure it was stable.

"What did you just say?" he asked.

"I asked if I could put the tray somewhere."

"No, before that."

"That tea helps you think. Shall I pour you some?" She was getting a sense of why, exactly, he needed help. Apparently his mind could only handle one thing at a time. There was also an undercurrent of panic, that he needed to find an anchor to help his world make sense again, but he didn't know where to start looking for it.

His brow wrinkled again. "But *when* does it help you think? Does it matter? Can it be ideally timed for maximum energy? And what of interruptions from trips to the water closet?"

"Professor!" She'd heard men say more vulgar things, but she had to at least pretend to be shocked. Part of her was intrigued, and the other felt she needed to steer him back to his tasks, both the one she was supposed to encourage him in and what he needed to do to heal emotionally.

"So I've heard you're working on a patent for an aether isolator?" she asked. He hadn't mentioned it the night before, but thanks to his explanation, she at least understood what it would do.

"Yes!" Now he smiled, and he looked like a delighted child.

"It's brilliant. Would you like to see the device? Well, the parts for it?"

"I'd love to," she said, and she was only half-pretending. She poured a cup of tea for him. "Let me take this tray back to the front."

"Please put a teaspoon of cream and half a sugar cube in there." He started scribbling on a piece of paper in front of him. "And the cream should be heated to…"

Pauline stifled another sigh as the tension from her shoulder crawled up her neck, and her head gave another throb. It was going to be a long day.

CHRISTOPHER HAD NEVER BEEN to Mrs. Reece's in the daytime before, so he had to plot a strategy before he left the townhouse.

Typically he would hire a cab to bring him. It would drop him off in a spot that would minimize the chance of being seen between the vehicle's door and the gate tucked into the high hedges around the house. But the men who drove the hired carriages and were paid well by the Madame were likely still asleep—they didn't start their runs until dusk—so he had to come up with a different way to make a discreet visit or wait until his usual hour. If he waited, the Madame would be busy.

What to do? He couldn't invite her to his house because his neighbors would talk.

"Does Your Grace know when he would like lunch?" Horace asked when he opened the door to the study.

Christopher dragged his attention back to the moment. "At the usual time, I suppose."

"Around one o'clock, then? Cook needs Smithy to take her to fetch more eggs, and she wanted to ensure she would have time to bake the quiche."

"I could eat later," Christopher said, irritation budding in his chest. Why didn't the man just come out and tell him the problem rather than playing these games?

"At around two o'clock, then? If Smithy takes her now, Cook said she could have it ready by one-thirty."

"One-thirty is fine." Christopher tried not to allow his impatience to show. Not for the first time, he felt irked at the domestic minutiae. Since her illness, his mother had stayed at the country house because the doctors recommended the fresher air, which left him to run things at the townhouse. Edward was certainly no help. He was polite to the servants but wasn't engaged enough in the mundane details of life to make decisions.

Perhaps the duchess was right—a wife would be helpful with this kind of thing.

"Where is Smithy?" Christopher asked. "In the garden?"

"I believe so. He and Cook are awaiting your word."

"I'll speak to him myself, but please tell Cook a late lunch will be fine."

Horace nodded but said nothing.

Christopher stifled his sigh and found the old gardener in the back tending to the townhouse's vegetable plot.

"Smithy, I have a strange request."

"Yes, sir?" The gardener stood and brushed his hands on his apron.

"I need to borrow a work shirt and trousers. And a hat, if you have one to spare."

Curiosity tented the older man's eyebrows, but he didn't inquire, only gestured to the room off the kitchen. "I have spares in there. It's my Sunday gig, less stained than the rest."

"Excellent, thank you. Oh, and if you could keep this between us, that would be grand."

"Yes, Your Grace."

Christopher waited until Smithy and Cook had left and

Horace was meeting with the head housekeeper over something—again, Christopher could see the benefit of having a wife to keep track of such things.

Attired in his borrowed clothing, he walked out of the back garden gate. His hat was pulled so low over his face he almost bumped into his new neighbor and, not wanting to be drawn into conversation, didn't look at him. Christopher only grunted a hello.

"Don't worry, Your Grace," the man's voice slithered after him. "I won't inquire as to where you're going in disguise in the middle of the morning."

4

———

M*iss Reece's Brothel, 5 July 1862*

THE LARGE HOUSE at the edge of town stood sedate and solid. It was gray stone like the others in the neighborhood, but much bigger and with high hedges around the yard in front and garden behind. No one walked along the street, but Christopher suspected others watched from the windows of the neighboring cottages. That was why he wore his disguise. Hopefully a man in work clothes visiting the ladies in the middle of the day wouldn't...

Oh, hell, what was he thinking? Of course it would make the neighbors wonder what sort of man needed to visit whores so badly he'd sneak off work and come in the middle of the day. He tugged his hat lower over his face and quickened his steps.

The front garden enveloped him with the scents of freshly pruned greenery and roses, and the trees that lined the walk provided shade and discretion. He slowed and allowed the breeze to envelop him, hopefully blowing away some of the perspiration. The clothes had been clean before he'd borrowed them, and now he wondered how he'd sneak them into the laundry to be cleaned so Smithy would have them for the following day.

Or he could just give the man money to buy new ones.

But then Horace, who watched the household accounts, would wonder.

What's the point of being the duke if I can't spend money how I please?

One of the younger girls opened the door. The darkness under her eyes shadowed the bright smile she attempted. Christopher guessed she hadn't had much sleep. Some of the regular patrons vied for the chance to have the younger women while they were still tight and before they'd been "spoiled" by too much sexual activity. He didn't envy the lot of these girls and always tried to ensure he paid Lucy enough that she could be choosy about who she serviced.

"We're not taking customers right now," she chirped.

Good God, how young was she? The corset she wore tried its best to plump up what little there was, but as Edward liked to remind Christopher in a different context, two times zero was still zero.

"I'm not here for that, Miss," he said. "Please tell Madame Reece someone needs to talk to her about information."

The girl's eyes widened, and she showed him into the parlor before bobbing a curtsey and rushing away.

The room looked different in the daytime. The curtains were mostly closed but let just enough sunlight in to show the wear on the cushions and scratches on the surfaces of the furniture from glasses set down too hard. He traced a filmy white ring with one finger.

"Candlelight is kind, Your Grace." Madame Reece glided

into the room. "There are reasons we practice our profession at night."

Like the parlor, she appeared shabby during the day. What the soft light showed as a youthful glow on her cheeks was revealed as rouge, which Christopher had known, but he'd bought into the illusion. Now he saw the spiderweb of wrinkles on her face and neck.

"Madame," Christopher said and bowed over her hand. "Thank you for seeing me at such an awkward time, but you look beautiful as ever."

"You're lying," she said.

He didn't contradict her, especially after seeing how young the girl who answered the door was. He wasn't sure who he was more irked with—her for putting a child in these circumstances or himself for allowing himself to be fooled for all these years. Whatever conspired, this would be his last visit to the place, and he would find some way to help these girls, especially the young ones.

"Thank you for seeing me," he said, figuring that was the safest route.

"When Giselle said a member of the gentry in gardener's clothing was in the parlor, I had to see who it could possibly be, and I recognized you immediately. Please, have a seat. Giselle will bring tea."

Christopher settled in a wingback chair that was wide enough for two people, likely intentionally. It swallowed him.

"How old is she?" The question burst from his lips.

"Twelve. She's Daisy's daughter. Why, have your tastes changed?"

"God, no. Twelve? She's working?"

"She's acting as a maid of all work at the moment, garnering interest among the patrons. I'll give her a coming out when she turns thirteen."

Christopher couldn't even look at the girl when she brought

the tea tray in, and his hand trembled when he lifted the cup. The way Madame Reece spoke of the girl's "coming out"—it was like a society debut, and for similar purposes, he couldn't help but think, but with the rough and immediate loss of innocence. He returned his teacup to the saucer, unable to drink.

"So about this information you wanted?" Madame Reece asked. Whereas before he'd seen her as a kind older woman, a mother figure to the girls in the house, now she seemed more a fairy-tale witch, the kind that baked children in an oven.

"Right, I am curious about a young woman in town, and all I can gather is that she's from the city. I know you have a network there."

Madame Reece nodded. "You're not the first to come by asking about a woman from the city, but the other gentleman was looking for someone who may not be here. What is the woman's name?"

"Pauline Danahue. She's working at the University, and I suspect she's low-born even though she's made efforts to hide it." Christopher found himself loath to mention too many details. Who else had been asking about her?

The woman placed a finger on her lips, the gesture more seductive than silencing, and pushed out a smile. "A man with means such as yours can surely afford to pay for an investigator. Why come to me?"

Here we go...

"I am seeking discretion, which I know you are the soul of. I assume you have some sort of system that allows you to rotate out the girls who haven't been able to cultivate regular customers." Christopher chose his words carefully so he wouldn't choke on them. "It's how you're able to get new girls in regularly."

"You're correct. I will make inquiries with my people in London." She paused and cocked her head.

Christopher extracted a bag of coins from his pocket. "This should be enough to get you started."

"Excellent, I shall do so immediately. More tea?"

He knew it was the polite thing to do, but his stomach turned at the idea of consuming anything there.

"Thank you, but I must be off. Cook is making one of her excellent quiches for lunch."

"Giselle will see you out."

After he left Madame Reece's, Christopher decided to stop by the university to see how Miss Danahue was getting along with Edward. From what he'd seen the night before, she should be fine, but he wanted to make sure.

Or maybe he wanted the excuse to see her again.

$$5$$

H*untington University, 5 July 1862*

AFTER THE DIMNESS of the brothel, the university felt bright and cheery, a world away.

Christopher found the secretary and Edward in Edward's office assembling some sort of contraption made of copper and glass spheres connected by tubing. Crates and the straw that had been used as packing material surrounded them. She had a strand in her hair, and Christopher resisted the urge to pluck it out. Edward stood by a table in his shirtsleeves and supervised her attaching a hose to a burner.

"That's it, make sure the connections are secure," Edward said. "We don't want the gas to leak out."

"Yes, Professor." She looked up and saw Christopher, and he hoped he saw more than relief in her smile. "Oh, Your Grace. You've returned."

Her brows drew together when she saw his attire.

Christopher looked down. Right, he'd forgotten he looked like a common laborer.

"Our cook is making one of her signature quiches for lunch," he said. "Would you like to join us?" He gestured to his clothing. "Obviously fancy dress isn't required."

Miss Danahue laughed, a true laugh. He preferred her open amusement to the simpering giggles he'd observed in other young women.

"Oh, quiche?" Edward straightened. "I had thought to work through lunch, but I can take a break." He brushed a sweaty strand of hair out of his face. The room was, indeed, stuffy.

"You need to go home and rest," Miss Danahue told him. "We can continue this tomorrow. Consider this a short workday for your data."

Christopher braced himself for Edward's objection and was surprised when his brother nodded. Since when had he become so docile?

"You're right. I need to see if napping in the afternoon will increase my productivity and focus. Let's just finish this part."

"What time should we be there?" Miss Danahue asked.

"For...?" Christopher reminded himself not to stare agape at how she handled Edward. What data? He would have to find out more at lunch. Oh, right, that's what she asked about. "At one thirty," he told her.

"I'll make sure he's there."

Christopher did pluck the straw from her hair. "I look forward to seeing both of you then."

When Christopher walked into the alley behind the town-house, he groaned. There, in front of him, was his mother's carriage. It had likely dropped her off at the front and then driven behind so the horses could be unhooked in the shade and given water in the small stable shed.

He unlatched the gate with deliberate movements and allowed it to swing in slowly so as not to alert the household to his return. Now all he had to do was cross the garden without anyone seeing him, and—

"Christopher?"

The duchess sat on a bench in the shade of a fig tree and stared at him with a most unladylike degree of astonishment, her teacup held halfway to her mouth. She pressed her lips together. Christopher felt as he had when he was a child and she'd caught him climbing that very tree, knocking off more figs than he picked.

Then her eyes crinkled, and she chuckled before asking, "I suppose I should inquire as to what you're doing in Smithy's Sunday attire."

Christopher pecked her on the cheek. "Sometimes it's easier to move about when people don't think you're the duke."

"Yes, that's what your father said. He kept some work clothing in the gardener's shed, but I suppose it's long been donated or turned to rags."

"Father would borrow the gardener's clothes?" Christopher couldn't imagine the old duke doing such a thing, even in the man's younger years.

"Yes, he was a man of many surprises, but I don't believe he did so after you were born. You coming along settled him down and helped him take his responsibilities more seriously." She waved him on. "Speaking of responsibilities, go change into your own clothing, and we can discuss the plans for the ball before lunch. Is your brother coming?"

"Yes, and one more guest." He deliberately didn't respond to her comment about responsibility.

"Oh?" She sipped her tea, her thin eyebrows raised flags of interest.

"I'll tell you about her in a moment."

"A *her*," she breathed. "And I thought your brother was done with women after Lily Cavender, but perhaps there's hope for him yet."

"Oh, no, not like that, Mother."

Her face tucked itself back into its usual prim lines, and he flinched from the disappointment it signaled.

"I just want to get you boys settled before..." She looked away.

"Don't talk like that. You'll outlast us all." Christopher pecked her on the cheek and escaped to his rooms. He didn't want to consider her mortality or that the next big event at the manor after the ball would likely be a funeral. They'd just been through it with their father, which was one reason Edward was so unsettled.

Or had been. Miss Danahue seemed to have pushed him in a promising direction.

He reached into the pocket of his borrowed trousers and extracted the piece of straw he'd pulled from her hair. He placed it on his vanity beside his own comb, and the golden color reflected in the silver of his grooming tools and warmed the entire tray.

Knowing that his father had also traipsed about the village in work clothes when he had been younger made Christopher feel better. He remembered the duke as being a somewhat dour man, but he and the duchess had always seemed in love. That was what Christopher wanted. Not love, necessarily, but a partnership. He suspected he wouldn't find that among the society misses—he'd encountered enough of them to know the only strategy they turned their heads to was how to land a title, or a better one, and be taken care of. And everyone wanted to wed a duke.

Like the girls at Miss Reece's always wanted to bed a duke. Either way, it was the same. Wed or bed, women didn't see him, only his title. Until today at Miss Reece's, he hadn't recognized how he'd played the game and only seen what was on the surface, using that to choose his bedmates. He should have realized it sooner, especially after what had happened with Edward and Lily Cavender.

Yes, wandering around in common clothing had been freeing, and his own attire felt tight and stuffy. He returned to the garden, and sweat sprang to his head when he walked outside.

"Aren't you warm?" he asked his mother.

She took his hand, and he found hers to be cold. "I'm always chilly nowadays," she said. "But if you're too hot, we can go in."

He sat. "No, I want you to be comfortable."

"Good. Then let's discuss the guest list for the ball. Of course word has gotten out, and everyone is clamoring for their daughters to come."

Now Christopher's perspiration had nothing to do with the heat and everything to do with his mother's strategy to see him married before she passed away.

PAULINE WALKED with the professor to the duke's townhouse. It felt good to be outside in the breeze, and she allowed herself to relax a smidgen. She hadn't felt the presence of whoever sought her since the previous night, although when they turned into the lane where the duke lived, a chill passed over her. She instinctively darted under the trees so she wouldn't be visible from any upper story windows. He wasn't there, but he had been recently. She struggled to remember the address on the flyer her landlady had shown her.

"Miss Danahue, are you all right?"

"I'm fine. I just like the trees," she said. "Where I come from, we don't have that many along the street." All of which was true except for the part about her being fine.

"Then you'll love our garden. We have a huge fig tree back there."

"I do like useful trees," she agreed, and he smiled.

A dour-looking butler let them in, and Pauline drew back from his supercilious examination. At the university, even though she was a secretary, she felt at least somewhat appreciated for her abilities. Now she felt every inch of her commonness and her failure to measure up to the metric of worthiness for entering the house.

The butler turned from her with a sniff and told Professor Bailey, "The duchess is here."

"Oh, mother. It will be good to see her. I want to tell her about the project Miss Danahue and I have concocted. Miss Danahue, this is Horace, our butler."

"Charmed," the butler said, although he was obviously not.

"Likewise," Pauline said with her most winning smile, daring him to sense she was as unimpressed by him as he was by her. She recognized the type—he'd be a deferential snob by day, but after dark when surrounded by women he paid to be near him, he'd pretend he was better than they, not that they all worked for a living. At least he got a decent wage.

The hallway was paneled with wood on the lower half of the walls, and Pauline wanted to run her fingers over the rich wallpaper pattern as she walked by. *Don't touch the wallpaper with dirty hands, Pauline,* she recalled someone saying, and there was a memory of having looked at a similar place from a lower position.

Then Horace's words sunk in. The duchess was there. Of course Pauline had heard of the formidable woman but had hoped never to face her. Now she would make her first impression disheveled and sweaty.

Pauline straightened her spine and drew her shoulders

back the way she'd seen her mother do thousands of times. *Don't let anyone make you believe you're less than they because of the accident of your birth,* she'd said with a wistful expression. *It only takes one misfortune, one mistake, to bring someone to lowly circumstances.*

Pauline couldn't imagine the duchess being brought to her mother's situation. She squinted against the light once they emerged from the gloom into the back garden. The professor ran to his mother, who took his hands but didn't stand. She said something Pauline couldn't hear, and Professor Bailey bent over. His mother kissed him on the cheek.

Pauline paused so as not to interrupt the reunion. She imagined the duchess wanted to see how her recently heartbroken son was doing.

The duke, back in his noble garb, sat beside his mother and watched as if to ensure his brother wouldn't accidentally harm her. The tender look on his face almost broke Pauline's heart because the hollowness at the woman's temples told her that black crepe would adorn the door and windows before the end of the summer. The duke looked up and saw Pauline, and she waved.

Professor Bailey gestured for Pauline to join them. "Oh, mother, you must meet Miss Danahue. She's helping me with unpacking my office and with assembling the aether isolator."

In spite of her ill health, the duchess speared Pauline with a clear gaze, and Pauline kept herself from breaking stride when their eyes met. Pauline sensed urgency from the woman, the need to see her boys settled and taken care of before she departed the earth. The baritone counterpoint to the sensation was the duke's wish to go at his own pace with finding a wife, which now came through clearly.

Pauline's disappointment surprised her. She should have known there was nothing behind his gesture that morning other than kindness.

The duchess took her hand. "Forgive me for not rising, my dear. I need to conserve my strength."

"I'm pleased to meet you, Your Grace," Pauline said.

"Likewise, my dear. Now tell me, has Edward been behaving himself?"

"Mother!" Professor Bailey turned pink from his collar to his hairline. "I am a distinguished scientist."

"And a twenty-year-old, barely a man. The youngest ever to be hired as university faculty." There was no dissembling in the duchess's wide grin, and Pauline smiled in return at the mother's pride. Then the duchess turned to Pauline.

"You know how young men are."

Now Pauline felt the duchess fishing for information. Had she been a governess? Something else? And yes, she did know how young men were. The prostitutes had complained about their lack of finesse often enough. She squashed the impulse to tell the truth just to see the shocked expression on the duchess's face.

"Professor Bailey is making brilliant progress," she said instead.

"Oh, good," the duke jumped in. "His chairman and dean will be happy. Shall we eat?"

The duchess waved him away. "I can get up and make it into the house myself. The two of you go ahead. Edward will stay close by in case I need him. Christopher, you escort Miss Danahue."

The duke held out an arm, and Pauline took it. Again, that strange disappointment that he would never give her his arm in any meaningful kind of way bubbled up. She swept it aside and reminded herself she needed to talk to him about paying her to babysit his brother. Twenty! No wonder he'd taken the heartbreak so hard—everything was magnified emotionally at that age, and she suspected he'd not had much practice navigating the treacherous social terrain of young relationships as a teenager.

Pauline and the duke walked ahead, and as soon as they were out of earshot, he leaned over and said, "She's pressing him for information about you."

"And why would she be doing that?" She tried not to sound cross.

"She's wondering if you might be a potential wife for Edward."

Pauline almost tripped, she was so startled. "I can assure you I have no such intentions. He's very young for his age."

"I'm aware of that, believe me." He shook his head. "That's part of the reason he ended up in the pickle with Lily Cavender. Mother is pushing us to marry. The thought hadn't crossed his mind until she suggested it, and of course the stupid girl thought she was snaring a duke."

"I still don't understand how she mistook him for you, especially after spending time with him."

Pain flickered over his face so quickly she thought she might have imagined it, replaced by his usual *forget seriousness* grin. "And do you want to spend time with me?"

Yes, please. But she reminded herself he liked to flirt and then turn around and do the opposite. She was too tired to play such games, and she was getting lightheaded from smelling the food, which made her head pound and her stomach shrink in on itself with hunger. "If it's too much trouble for me to be here, I can leave."

And pretend I have enough money to buy something to eat.

Then the sensation that *he* was somewhere nearby overtook her, perhaps as close as on the other side of the townhouse wall and small service alley that separated the estates.

But I can't leave.

6

____

D*uke of Waltham's Townhouse, 5 July 1862*

PERPLEXED by the coldness that had frosted her tone, Christopher stopped just outside the dining room and steered Miss Danahue into the parlor.

"I'm sorry, did I say something to offend you?"

She jerked away from him and stumbled, catching herself on the back of an armchair with both arms. Her dark eyelashes stood out against her suddenly pale cheeks. "I'm not feeling well."

"I can see that. Should I send for a physician?"

"Or a carriage to bring me home." Her tone said she would rather not take that option, and he thrilled at the thought that she'd rather stay here and allow him to take care of her.

And why not? She was doing him a favor by watching over Edward. Which reminded him...

"Once you're up to it, we can discuss the extra compensation you deserve for keeping Edward on task."

"Fine."

He'd had enough experience with women to know that "fine" usually meant it wasn't, and he cursed his clumsiness.

"I'm sorry, Your Grace." His formal title put even more distance between them. "I'm overwrought. I don't like being a helpless female, and I don't need the aid of your physician. I'm sure I will be all right after I eat something."

"Allow me to fetch a plate for you."

"I can eat with you, the duchess, and the professor." But she swayed when she released the chair and stood upright.

He guided her around the chair and pressed her to sit in it. "I'll be right back. No point in you fainting on the way to the dining room. Then we'd have to find a bed for you." He left before she could protest.

His mother and Edward already had plates in front of them, Edward's full of the quiche and roast chicken and his mother's more than half empty.

"You need to eat more than that, Mother."

She laughed. "I like this mother hen side of you, Christopher. How is Miss Danahue? I didn't take her for the type to lure a duke into a parlor by feigning illness."

"She's a sensible young woman, but you know how Edward gets when he's involved in something." Christopher picked up both the remaining plates on the table along with the silverware and napkins. "I believe she is truly hungry and possibly dehydrated from being in Edward's stuffy office most of the day. We'll be eating in the parlor, where it's cooler."

Edward only shrugged, and a footman filled his lemonade glass with the last of the pitcher and disappeared into the kitchen.

"Please send one of the footmen in with some lemonade for Miss Danahue and me."

"Give Miss Danahue my regards," the duchess said. "She's the first young woman I know of who's captured that much attention from you. Remember, you need to pick a wife who is of your station. We still know nothing about Edward's secretary."

"I'm working on it. Sometimes people have secrets they want to keep for good reason."

"Now you're thinking like a fairy tale hero." She waved her fork at him. "Go, take her lunch. We can discuss the invitation list after my nap."

Christopher found Miss Danahue in the same chair—good, she hadn't bolted—with her head propped on one hand and eyes closed. A little line between her brows told him she still didn't feel well. He put the plates on the end table, and she opened her eyes.

"That smells divine."

"Our cook is known for her quiches. She trained in France during one of the brief windows when we were getting along with them."

He handed her a napkin and some silver, and once she'd spread the napkin on her lap, the plate. She waited for him to get settled, but he gestured for her to start.

"The footman will be bringing in some lemonade. While I appreciate the seriousness with which you approach your task of supervising Edward, it doesn't mean you should neglect your own needs. He tends to forget others don't focus to the exclusion of all else like he does."

He was pleased when she took a small bite of the Quiche Lorraine and her eyes closed with pleasure. He had the same reaction he'd had that morning when he saw her lick the crumbs from her palm and was glad he'd just settled with the napkin and plate on his lap. It would be a lucky man to bring that look to her face in bed. He suspected she wouldn't limit bedroom activities to making babies but would rather enjoy it.

And why was he thinking about her in bed? He turned his attention to the silky quiche but kept sneaking glances at her. Lemonade appeared, and once she'd eaten—finished everything on her plate with gusto, another difference between her and the delicate misses he typically interacted with—the color had returned to her cheeks, and the little line smoothed from her brow.

"You look like you're feeling better," he said once the plates were cleared.

"Much, thank you." She sipped the lemonade slowly, as though savoring it. "You're right—I should have paid more attention to how I was feeling."

She still looked at him with some wariness, which irked him. Yes, it was his fault she was stuck babysitting Edward, but what had he done to deserve this distance she insisted on putting between them?

Ah, right, there was the question of money.

"And I shouldn't have assumed you'd be willing to take on this task without asking you first." He scooted his chair closer to her so he could lower his voice. He didn't know what his mother would think, but he suspected that offering a young lady money in any context wouldn't feel proper to the duchess.

"It's quite all right, and I'm glad you brought up the idea of extra compensation." She took a deep breath and pressed her lips together for a moment before continuing. "I'm going to have to stay late to take care of my university duties, and I was hoping we could work something out. As you mentioned, dealing with the professor isn't exactly easy."

If offering her money wasn't proper, her asking for it before he brought it up again was downright shocking. Christopher had to again remind himself that she wasn't the type of woman he was used to. In fact, this request confirmed she'd come from the working class, and unexpected disappointment tweaked his gut.

But why was he disappointed? She fascinated him, but he knew they couldn't be any more than, well, whatever they were. A man and woman who enjoyed each other's company in a completely innocent—*damn it*—way.

"I'm sorry, Your Grace. I've offended you." She stood.

He rose as well and put a hand on her arm. "No, you just surprised me, that's all. And I agree—you deserve something extra for taking on this challenge with my brother."

The tension fell from her and left a dazzling smile in its wake. There was that disappointment again—she was so beautiful. And intelligent. And determined. And everything else that would be perfect for his future duchess, if only she came from a good family.

Still, noblemen had married commoners before to help strengthen the bloodline. If she came from a respectable trade family, he was sure they could work something out. He only needed to see if she was fine with exploring this possibility further.

"Thank you, Your Grace. I was thinking an extra shilling per week would be reasonable."

"I was going to give you five."

Her eyebrows rose. "That's very generous. Or is your brother going to spring more surprises on me that I'm unaware of?"

He laughed. Damnit, she had a sense of humor, too. "No, but I do want you to have the resources to get something to eat and drink on campus if he makes you work through lunch."

"Thank you, Your Grace," she said again, and he cringed at the sound of his title coming from her delectable lips. Every time she used it, he felt the distance between them.

"Call me Christopher," he said. "Since we're business partners, after all." It was a shabby reason, but if he were to implement his plan, he needed familiarity, not formality.

"All right, Christopher." She rolled his name over her

tongue like it was a hard candy, and he almost had to sit down again.

"And what may I call you?" he prompted, his voice low. He knew he must be looking at her like she was a particularly attractive morsel, but he couldn't help it. He couldn't take his eyes from her lips. When she ran her tongue over them, it sent a jolt of hungry pleasure through him.

"You may call me Pauline. When we're alone."

She shifted to turn away from him, and he fought the urge to clasp her tighter and draw her closer. She walked to the window and rubbed her arms like she was cold. He felt the opposite. Being near her drew him in, like a fire on a night when a man doesn't feel the cold until he finds comforting flames.

"So you feel that an extra five shillings a week is reasonable?" he asked. He stood beside her. She only peeked around the edge of the curtain, and he was selfishly glad that only he would see her beauty in the soft light coming through the trees outside.

"It's very generous, Your—Christopher."

"I do have one more thing to ask of you. It will be our secret."

She surprised him by snorting. "And here we go," she sighed.

"What?" he asked.

"Some sort of indecent arrangement, perhaps? I should have known that no duke would spend his money without getting something extra in return."

Christopher took offense for a moment before reeling in his shock that she would think such a thing. The plight of the poor girl at Madame Reece's had reminded him of what a delicate position women who needed to make a living were in. He couldn't blame Pauline for being insulted. There was no telling what she'd encountered from men who would feel their title gave them permission to take what they wanted from a common woman. He'd show her he was different.

"No, nothing like that," he said. "As you've probably noticed, my mother is rather eager to see me and Edward settled. She's not well."

Pauline nodded. "I'm very sorry for that. It seems that you and Professor Bailey are close to her."

"I don't want her overexerting herself with this stupid ball she insists upon throwing. Would you be willing to pose as my betrothed so she can drop the ridiculous venture?"

He wasn't sure what he expected her to do—swoon, throw herself into his arms, become even more insulted.

What he didn't anticipate was the very unladylike guffaw of laughter she let out. It was infectious, though. Soon he joined her, and they collapsed into each other's arms laughing like they'd heard the most marvelous joke.

Before he realized what he was doing, he caught her lips with his mouth and tasted the salt of their mingled tears. She stiffened but didn't pull away, and he gently guided her to him, where she fit like she'd been made for him.

I'M KISSING THE DUKE!

Or, rather, he was kissing her. Pauline didn't know what had just happened, only that he'd made a ridiculous suggestion—she couldn't pose as his betrothed, it would only bring her to the attention of the man who hunted her. And she'd been so relieved that the duke—*Christopher*—wasn't propositioning her, at least not for sex.

Or would that come later? Her body was telling her it wouldn't mind one bit seeing and experiencing the noble naughty bits. She bet he was hung like a—

With a regretful sigh, she pulled her lips away from his. She couldn't start thinking like a whore or he would treat her like one, and she dampened that part of her that wanted to find out what it would be like. Her rebellious legs shook, and she had to lean into him, reminding herself not to get too used to enjoying his solid strength. Or his broad chest and shoulders. Or the hard abdominal muscles she could feel beneath her hands.

Or his massive erection that pressed into her stomach.

Damn it. She flatted her hands against his chest and pushed herself away with every ounce of will. Of course she moved and he, being a solid wall of tempting muscle, didn't.

"It's rather unseemly to kiss a girl before she's accepted your proposal," she said, her cheeks heating at the breathiness of her voice.

"I just wanted to ensure you'd say yes," he said, his own tones low enough to vibrate something needy in her core.

A dark shadow outside caught her eye. She couldn't see details through the sheer fabric covering the window, but it looked like a man in a dark hat approached the house. Her own emotions were so befuddled she couldn't sort out what the man outside felt or whether he was the one who threatened her. She stepped back into the relative gloom of the parlor.

"And what do you say?" he asked.

Three knocks sounded on the front door. The noises jolted through Pauline, reminding her the past would always be just one step behind her.

"I can't pretend to be your fiancée, Christopher. You know nothing about me, about my background or where I come from. This farce would only break your mother's heart."

The butler's footsteps echoed through the hallway, and the creak of the front door made Pauline catch her breath with panic. A gentle finger lifting her chin made it subside, and she opened her eyes to see the concerned face of the duke gazing down at her.

"What don't I know about you?" he asked. "You come from

working stock—that much I can tell, but stranger matches have been made."

Than a duke with the daughter of a whore? She couldn't say it, couldn't shatter this moment. She opened her mouth to object again on general terms, but the butler cleared his throat from the doorway.

"Your Grace? There's a young man at the door. He said he's looking for a young lady who fits Miss Danahue's description."

Pauline swallowed the strangled, panicked sound her throat wanted to make.

"I'll speak with him. Stay here," Christopher told her. As soon as he walked into the hall, Pauline looked at the butler, who gazed at her with even more disdain than when she'd entered.

"I should go," she said.

"I agree," the butler replied. "I'll show you the way out through the kitchen. There's a door on the other side of the room that leads into the dining hall. Your things are in the cloak room."

Pauline followed him, irked that he implied she wasn't good enough for the duke even though she'd thought the same only a few moments before.

The butler returned her reticule and bonnet and let her out into the garden. She darted across it and to the gate, not feeling safe until she'd closed it and reached the alley. Even then, her relief was short-lived. As she tied her bonnet ribbons, she felt *him* searching for her, and he was nearby. Had he been the man at the front door? She hadn't gotten a good look at him.

There was nothing ladylike about how she lifted her skirts and fled. Pauline's mind worked as quickly as her feet. She would have to see the week out, hide as much as possible, collect her first payment from the duke, and be on her way.

Christopher met the young man in the study. He had the wholesome look of an English country squire with the freckles of a laborer. On a second look, Christopher noted the keen intelligence in the man's eyes, how he took in every inch of his surroundings.

"Can I assist you?" Christopher asked. "I understand you're looking for someone." He hadn't missed Pauline's anxious reaction, and he was curious. Did she need protecting?

"I'm Inspector Henry Davidson," the young man said. They shook hands before the inspector continued, "I'm looking for a certain young woman."

"Aren't we all?" Christopher replied.

The inspector acknowledged Christopher's attempt at a joke with a smile and tilt of his head. He reached into his breast pocket and pulled out a folded piece of paper. "I've not seen her, but this is a sketch made from descriptions by those who know her."

The young woman in the picture could have been Pauline. There was something off about the eyes, and the lips definitely weren't right. Christopher could vouch for their shape and taste in detail. But there was enough similarity that he needed to know more.

"Why are you looking for her?"

"So you've seen her?" Davidson arched an eyebrow in a way that made Christopher wonder exactly what he was implying.

"I don't know. I've seen many dark-haired young women. She looks familiar, but I can't say with certainty." He handed the drawing back to the inspector. "Is she dangerous?"

"No, but she's in danger. Her mother was killed in a brothel in London, and we think the murderer is after the daughter."

The bookcases grew taller as Christopher's stomach—and butt—dropped into the chair behind him. "A brothel?"

"Yes, the mother was a much sought-after courtesan, particularly by the nobles in town for the Season."

Christopher wanted to clutch his hands over the knot of disappointment that drew his guts tighter. "And was the daughter...?" He couldn't bring himself to say it.

"She lived at the brothel, which employs women younger than she for men who have the taste for them. I cannot say for certain, but there's a chance."

"I see." Pauline was certainly old enough.

Davidson handed Christopher a card. "If you do happen to see her, here is my contact information. Please tell her to find me. I need her to act as a witness to catch and convict her mother's killer, and there is someone else who seeks her, although I'm not at liberty to say who."

Christopher took the card and nodded. He couldn't speak around the stomach acid that had flooded his throat.

Pauline, a prostitute? Now possessiveness warred with disappointment and disgust.

"I'll let myself out."

Of course Davidson would know that Pauline had been there, that Christopher knew her. He'd done a shabby job of hiding it. For a moment he felt relieved that she had rejected his proposal, but then concern for her overcame his ignoble impulse. She was still looking after Edward, who seemed to be developing a fondness for her. If something happened to her, it might set Edward back. There was no telling how precarious his current state was.

But there had been something innocent about her kiss. Although she had enthusiasm—that made him smile—and talent—now he frowned again—she certainly hadn't kissed like an experienced woman. He was embarrassed to admit to himself he could be a connoisseur of kisses.

She'd also thought he was improperly propositioning her and had warned him there was something untoward in her past. Would she have told him had they not been interrupted?

Christopher rose and shook his head to clear the ringing in

his ears. Davidson's revelation had knocked him flat, like a skilled prizefighter who had an opponent's feet out from under him before the second punch.

Even so, the picture might *not* have been of her. He could be manufacturing anxieties. He'd go ask her immediately and clear things up, find out she was a daughter of a tinkerer or barrister, not of a whore.

When he reached the parlor, he found it empty except for Horace, who cleared their lunch dishes.

"Where is Miss Danahue?"

"The young lady was called away."

"You mean she left."

"Yes, Your Grace. And in quite a rush, too."

Rather than the revelation he'd hoped for, Christopher was faced with more evidence that there was something amiss about Miss Pauline Danahue. The question was, what was he to do about it?

"Oh, and Your Grace, your mother is resting but wants to go over the guest list for the ball at tea."

CHRISTOPHER STEWED over the Pauline Danahue problem, as he'd started calling it in his mind, all through the following day, which was Sunday. To make things worse, Edward was moping again and refused to leave his room or accompany them to church, which put his mother in a cranky state until she got into public.

Christopher noticed the church was full for a summer day, when most families would be at their country estates. He realized what the draw was after the service, when a parade of mothers and daughters came to greet him and his mother. It was obvious all were hopeful for an invitation to the coveted ball. After Christopher's polite smile had tensed itself into an almost grimace, earning a reprimand from his mother, he pleaded off to rest before lunch.

When he walked into his room, he found his footman arranging his vanity. The piece of straw was missing.

"Where is the straw that was on the tray?" he asked.

"I threw it out, Your Grace. I'm sorry, I don't know how that piece of grass got in here."

Christopher looked at his implements, which seemed a dull, lifeless shade now. "That's all right, Jonathan. I was saving it, but it's probably not important now."

"Doing experiments like Lord Edward, then? Your mother's a lucky lady to have two such clever sons."

Hardly.

He dismissed the footman and sat on the window seat, which overlooked the street in front of the townhouse. He used to spend hours there, reading and dreaming about what his life would be like when he was a duke. His current state, at age twenty-three, hardly lived up to his expectations, particularly as he'd always imagined a duchess beside him, but not until he'd had a bit of excitement first.

The mystery of Pauline Danahue provided excitement, but not the type he'd hoped for. He surprised himself by acknowledging he wasn't sure anymore what he wanted, only that he needed to elude his mother's marital trap lest he suffocate in a marriage to the wrong woman.

Movement below caught his attention, and he saw his mysterious new neighbor walk up the street, stop in front of Christopher's front step, and look up at the house. His face was shadowed by his hat, but Christopher recognized his wavy dark hair. The neighbor paused like he thought about ringing the doorbell, then ducked into the alley between the houses.

Christopher frowned—what was the man doing?

Then Inspector Davidson came along. He, too, paused in

front of the house, but only briefly, and then he kept going. The neighbor popped out of the alley and dashed up his own steps.

That was odd.

Christopher went downstairs to watch the street from the parlor in case anything else interesting happened.

"Ah, Christopher, there you are," his mother said. "We need to finalize this guest list."

"I thought we already had?"

"That was until that pitiful parade happened after church today. Now, who do you think seemed too desperate? I won't have your brother put in danger of heartbreak again, and one of them might decide at the ball that if she can't have you, she'll go after him, the brother of a duke standing to inherit if something happens to you before you have heirs. At least these girls will have the sense to know which is which..."

Christopher cringed again at the reminder that Edward's state was his fault. Whatever Miss Danahue's past might be, he owed her for helping to manage the aftermath of his mistake. Plus, he didn't want to be responsible for Edward should he lose his university position. Edward's refusal to get out of bed if he couldn't go work—which the duchess wouldn't allow him to do with it being the Sabbath—indicated his continued fragile emotional state.

A touch on his arm brought Christopher out of his dark thoughts.

"I know you're not enthused about the ball," the duchess told him, "but it will be my farewell bow to society, and I want it to go well and for you to have a set path to being settled after. This situation with Edward has affected you, no matter what you happen to think about it."

Christopher wanted to refute her words, but she gripped his wrist with less strength than she'd had the day before and the day before that and the day before that. He'd already failed Edward. He could at least do this for her.

"Then let's discuss it. We should finalize the details considering it's in six days. The invitations should go out tomorrow."

Her smile almost erased the frail fatigue that deepened the lines on her face. "And we need a theme. I've always loved the Cinderella legend, the rags to riches tale of the cast-aside daughter of a duke."

He squeezed her hand. "You were always a romantic."

He thought of Miss Danahue, how she'd fled the day before. She hadn't left a shoe behind, only a string of suspicions and questions, which he intended to find answers to.

7

———

 *etherics Department, Huntington University, 8 July 1862*

THE NEXT DAY, Pauline showed up to work as usual. She'd tried to tell herself she wasn't spooked by the events of Saturday, but she'd spent all of Sunday hidden in her rooms, which were stuffy and close in the heat. Opening the window only let in all the unpleasant summer smells from outside.

Then she'd not slept well due to nightmares about her mother's death. She'd only seen the back of the murderer, but it had been enough. The feeling of the dream clung to her, and she shied away from every long morning shadow in her path. If anything, the events of Saturday had proven that she could not spend any more time than necessary with the duke. Her duty was to Professor Bailey, whom she found in a particularly petulant mood when she arrived.

"All my progress is lost because I had to take the stupid Sabbath day off," he grumbled. "I couldn't work, so all I could do was think. And I didn't like my thoughts, which have always been brilliant. Stupid emotions—I hate them."

"You and me both." She put a hand to her shoulder, which had recommenced its throbbing, and rubbed the top of it. *Think. If he doesn't make progress, the duke won't pay you.* "Or this is an opportunity to see whether your regimen will hold after a break. Every good scientist needs breaks."

He glanced up from the papers on his desk. "You're right. I should see if I can maintain my momentum and make adjustments if not. Now, what did we start with on Saturday?"

Her shoulder twinged at the thought of carrying the tray down the hall again, but she said, "I believe it was tea."

He checked his watch. "We're already behind. The tea please, Miss Danahue."

WHEN CHRISTOPHER ARRIVED at the Department of Aetherics, he found the building mostly deserted. He wasn't surprised— the academics of the town scattered during the summer, taking the opportunity to go south to the beach or to the continent to do research. He'd heard the university was looking into starting a new geology/archaeology department, but it was still in the exploration stage. They'd already approached him for money, though, with a hint that it could be named after his late father if he was the primary donor.

Edward needs to stay employed first. Then we'll see.

He liked supporting the university and charities, and he tolerated the bookkeeping, but he had little patience for dealing with people.

That thought brought his mother's ball to mind, and he couldn't help but think it was a good thing Pauline hadn't accepted his invitation to pose as his betrothed. Finding out her son was going to marry a woman who was—could be—the daughter of a whore would have killed his mother sooner. Another ruse that could have blown up in his face in a tragic way, and Pauline had unwittingly saved him again.

That's the kind of duchess I need—someone who doesn't only think of herself.

He found another girl at the front desk. She didn't do anything, just sat with her hands folded and watched him approach.

"Welcome to the Department of Aetherics," she chirped when he stopped in front of her. "How can I help you?"

"Where is Miss Danahue?" he asked. The girl looked very young.

"Helping Professor Bailey with a special project." She inclined her head toward the corridor leading to Edward's office. "I'm just filling in until they're done."

"Thank you."

He turned to head that way, but she said, "Stop! They aren't to be interrupted. Chairman Kluge said so, and I already got in trouble once for bringing a message in."

Her bright smile had disappeared, and her lips now drew together in a disapproving moue.

"I'm his brother. My mother sent me to check up on him." It was only half a lie. His mother had said she wanted to know what magic Miss Danahue used to get Edward to stop his heartbroken moping. How else was he to find out?

"Oh, you're the duke!" She brightened again. "The first thing I heard about when I arrived in town was that you're giving a ball. Or your mother is. Because she's—" She clamped her mouth shut.

Christopher would have been offended had he not been fighting the urge to pat her on the head like one would a yappy puppy.

"Yes, and you may come if you like, but only if you allow me to see my brother and don't tell the chairman."

She nodded and mimed locking her lips with a key.

"And your name?" he asked. "I need it for the list."

She mimed unlocking her lips. "Eugenia Wills."

He repeated it so he'd remember. "I'll add you. Thank you."

She locked her lips again and nodded. He wondered how long she'd keep her mouth shut and if she would mime turning the little key again before speaking to someone else.

He walked toward Edward's office and kept his footfalls silent and ears alert for conversation. The door was cracked, and he peered in.

The sight made him bite back a cry of dismay. Pauline and Edward sat on the floor, and she held him while he sobbed on her shoulder. He hadn't known their relationship was so...intimate.

He must have made some noise because she looked up, and her face flushed when their eyes met.

"Help," she mouthed.

"What happened?" he asked and entered.

Pauline pried a card from Edward's hand and gave it to Christopher. He scanned it, then read it slowly.

Dearest Edward, I am so sorry for the way I treated you. Please forgive me and escort me to your family's ball at the end of the week. Devotedly, Lily.

"That little minx," he muttered. "What do you want to bet that she heard about the ball, that she wasn't invited, and decided to do anything to get into it?"

"It's turning into the social event of the season, and Edward is the most vulnerable of your family."

Edward had subsided to sniffles. "I can't stand it," he moaned. "Why does she toy with my affections like this?"

Christopher helped his brother to stand and moved him to sit at the desk. Then he turned to help Pauline up but found she'd already stood and was brushing packing straw from her skirt. Goodness, the stuff was everywhere. He gestured for her to follow him into the hallway.

"Twenty is still a tender age for some," she said.

"You can't be much older than that," Christopher told her. His mother's training kicked in, then, or at least her example of taking the opportunity to fish for information. "Have you encountered many young men like him?"

"A few. Thank you for coming in—I don't know how I would have snapped him out of it if you hadn't. My usual tricks weren't working."

"Which are...?"

"Getting him busy with something. Oh!" She looked at the small watch on the chain around her neck. "It's past his mid-morning tea time."

The timepiece caught Christopher's attention. It was a pocket watch with a filigree butterfly for a cover. "That's beautiful." He shook his head. "But that doesn't matter. Fetch him some tea, please."

She nodded and dashed toward the main office. "Genie, is the water hot?"

Christopher returned to the office, where Edward sat at the window and looked outside. A tendril of ivy waved in the breeze, and Edward watched it, seemingly mesmerized.

"Come now, Edward," Christopher said. "Buck up. Don't worry, we shall not invite her. In fact, we'll have a footman standing by to remove her on sight should she have the audacity to show up."

With a nod, Edward sniffled again, and Christopher gave him a handkerchief.

"Miss Danahue must think me an idiot," Edward said. He looked at Christopher with rare shrewdness. "I know that you and Kluge are having her watch me so I finish the aether isolater."

"It's your first major heartbreak," Christopher said. It would have happened eventually, right? He couldn't take all the blame. "And you've never done well when your emotions overrule your head."

"I've had enough grief." Edward looked up at his brother. "With Father dying and now Mother..."

Christopher wanted to retreat from the intensity of the pain in Edward's eyes, but he stayed and put a hand on his brother's shoulder. With Edward's university position and intelligence, it was easy to forget that he was still young and that Christopher would be responsible for watching over Edward until he found his own wife.

Perhaps Mother is right. Perhaps I need to find a wife to push me to take that final step toward growing up.

"I'm here for you."

Pauline entered carrying a tea tray. Christopher noticed the compressed line of her lips and the stiff way she held her right shoulder. He relieved her of the tray and placed it on the desk. She smiled but winced when she lifted the full teapot. She set it down.

"This probably needs to steep a few more minutes," she said.

"Are you all right?" Christopher asked.

She rolled her right shoulder and tilted her head to the left. "I'm just tight this morning. Please don't concern yourself with it."

"Of course I'm going to concern myself with it." But what could he do? He was an unmarried man, and she an unmarried woman, and—

What the hell? He'd already kissed her.

"Have a seat." He held out the chair on the other side of the desk for her. She sat, and he kneaded her shoulder. Even under her clothing, the knot beside her shoulder blade was palpable, as was the rope of tension across her upper back. When he reached her neck, she hissed.

"What?"

"An old injury. Don't worry about it."

"Of course I'm worried about it," he said. He noticed how he echoed her words again, but a flash of anger replaced his bewilderment at his apparent lack of original thought. "Did someone do this to you?" He reduced the strength with which he massaged her neck, but he continued in spite of the way his stomach twisted when he thought of another man's hands on her.

"Mmmm, that's it. An old injury, that's all. From a previous life I'd rather not discuss."

Christopher noticed the evasion but didn't press. That was one piece of potential evidence for her past as a prostitute, and he told himself he didn't want Edward to be shocked about his caregiver.

Edward poured the tea and even used the strainer, which he tended to forget. "How do you take your tea, Miss Danahue?"

She tried to stand, but Christopher kept her in the chair with gentle hands on her shoulders. "I'm not done yet."

"But I only brought two cups."

"For you and Edward, then. I've already had enough this morning."

"That's not very English of you," she teased, but she didn't move. This time when she tilted her head left, something in her shoulder made a popping sound. "Ah, that's much better. And I take my tea black."

Christopher hadn't known any noble women who drank their tea without milk when it was available. Damn, there was another tic in the *former whore*, or at least lowborn commoner column. Disappointment didn't stop his hands from working, however. It was satisfying to feel her relax under his touch. It was obvious she hadn't been cared for by someone in a long time, and he wasn't going to leave until he had found and conquered every knot in her neck and shoulders.

If it meant he got to admire her glossy dark hair and the curve of her breasts from above, he wouldn't complain.

Edward shook his head and soon lost himself in his notes, leaving Christopher to concentrate on his own task.

"I think you've done it," she murmured about twenty minutes later. She still sat straight—her corset wouldn't allow otherwise—but the curve of her shoulders was even on both sides and relaxed, and she could tilt her head without wincing.

"I could send you to our physician," Christopher offered. "He might have something else to suggest."

"Thank you, but I'll be fine." She rose. "Plus your brother and I have work to do."

He felt the dismissal. "Take it easy, and no heavy lifting. Edward can do that."

Edward looked up from the diagrams he studied and nodded. His eyes had brightened, and Christopher felt he'd passed the crisis point, although there was likely more to come.

"Yes, Your—"

He held up a finger.

"Christopher," she said, and she looked away, her cheeks flushed.

He resisted the urge to peck her on the cheek. It would be innocent compared to their kiss in the parlor from Saturday, but he was mindful of their audience, and he'd already blasted through enough social conventions by massaging her.

"I'll return to check on you." He stopped before admonishing her to be careful how she slept. He'd been thrown by his father's horse Lucifer more than once, and it had only been the capable hands of the family physician that had saved him from a long-term injury similar to hers. He also remembered the fortresses of pillows he'd built to keep him from rolling on to the hurt side.

Perhaps her injury was also riding-related, but then why would she have evaded his question?

"I appreciate your help," she said.

Edward had brought his diagrams to the open crates and studied them with an intensity Christopher recognized as impenetrable, so he did indulge in a kiss on one of her high cheekbones that left his lips tingling. Her blush deepened, but she swatted him.

"Go on now, we have work to do."

He bowed to her and left, but he couldn't hide his grin. He held the memory of her shoulders under his hands as long as he could.

~

AETHERICS DEPARTMENT, *11 July, 1862*

CHRISTOPHER KNEW that Edward was getting close to isolating the aether with Pauline's help. She kept him on track by encouraging him to model his life according to scientific principles of order, structure, and predictability. As proud as he was of Edward's looming accomplishment, Christopher knew he'd have to return to his pattern of rare visits to the department. Otherwise, he'd arouse suspicion of wanting to marry the beautiful secretary.

Or bed her, which would be what other young men of his situation would do.

The response his body had to being around her left no doubt that he did, but he also wanted her to come to bed with him willingly. But he didn't want to ruin her. If she wasn't already.

The arguments with himself made him want to tear his hair out. When they were apart, he convinced himself that they couldn't be together—her past was too suspect. But when he saw her smile, noticed how she held her lips when deep in thought, and heard her laugh, he wanted to allow for the possibility of some sort of relationship. But he couldn't turn her into his whore. He couldn't use another woman like that and keep what shred of respect he still had for himself after what he'd done to Edward.

There was one thing he was certain of. His conversations with Inspector Davidson—and there had been others—continued to convince him there was something amiss about Pauline, but he couldn't accept she was a former prostitute. Christopher didn't want to hand her over to Davidson, but if she was in danger, he wanted her to know, and he didn't question his need to protect her. She'd done so much for them. And he needed to find some clever way to discover what her background was, as it was in poor taste to directly ask if her mother was a whore. If he was wrong, he'd insult her so thoroughly she would have to turn him away, and he didn't want to ruin whatever slight chance there might be of bedding or wedding her.

Miss Reece hadn't found any useful information from her London contacts aside from that they were relieved that a serial whore killer seemed to have moved on from their midst. It seemed that only increased the danger Pauline was in, so in desperation, Christopher turned to his mother. She had continued to be curious about Miss Danahue, and he'd finally had to break down and tell her everything, including his conversations with Inspector Davidson.

Well, almost everything. He kept their kisses to himself.

"I knew there was something off about the girl," she said. She wrapped her hands around her teacup, which she only took occasional sips from. Her eyes had turned a yellowish color, and her lips took on a blue cast if she exerted herself even slightly. Even Edward had noticed her decline and requested that she give up the idea of the ball, but she persisted.

"Yes, but she's done wonders for Edward." Christopher put

his teacup back on its saucer. The air was too warm for him to want to heat his insides. "She knows just how to handle him."

"And is there any affection between them? Sometimes the end of a bad relationship can lead an inexperienced young man into a worse one."

"None. She treats him as a little brother, and he acts toward her as one would toward a competent assistant, nothing more."

"That's good. And how do you feel about her?" The duchess blinked over the rim of her teacup, and Christopher reminded himself that although her body failed her, her mind was as sharp as ever. Although he'd been able to leave out bits of the truth, he couldn't lie to her.

"I will admit I'm somewhat taken with her."

"Only somewhat?" She raised her eyebrows. "She is the first woman I've ever seen you give so much attention. If she is the daughter of a whore, it is unfortunate for both of you, but there are other arrangements. I just wish I could figure out why she looks so familiar."

Shock at his mother's suggestion—was she really saying he could take Pauline as a lover if he had to marry someone else? —made Christopher speechless.

"Don't look at me agog like that. Do you think I am a complete innocent? Why do you think your father snuck about in laborer's clothing? He had someone on the side, although I never found out who."

"But you two seemed so much in love." Of course Christopher knew his father had patronized Mrs. Reece's on occasion, but it was something all men of the era did, or at least the noble ones.

Hearing he'd actually had a mistress, though...

"We were." She placed the teacup on its saucer, and he poured more tea. She waited for him to finish and then held his eyes. "But there was another he loved just as much. He was always the soul of discretion, and he treated me and you boys well, but I could tell I didn't have his entire heart. That's why I hope you find out that Miss Danahue comes from good stock. It is possible for a man's heart to be divided in two, but it will send him to an early grave."

"Like Father." The physicians had only told them that the duke's heart had given out one day while he was out riding.

But what—or who—had he been riding? Christopher shook his head against the thought.

"Yes, like your father." She put a hand over her middle with a grimace. "And I will acknowledge that missing him is part of why I'm only fighting so hard. I want to join him and ask him who she was and why I wasn't enough."

Christopher's head spun from the revelations. "It hardly seems fair."

"No, it's not fair. You have a responsibility to your bloodline, as he did. Our age is somewhat more progressive with regard to mingling of noble and common, but there are some things that cannot be allowed, like the marriage of a duke and a whore's daughter. Consequently, other arrangements, although less than ideal, are necessary."

He couldn't take any more of this conversation. "Would you like some laudanum?"

She nodded. "Yes, dear. I will rest for the morning. Bring the young lady for lunch. Sometimes it takes a woman to get to the bottom of what's going on with another woman."

PAULINE DIDN'T WANT to hope that the duke would come back and knead the tension from her neck and shoulders with his strong hands. Or sneak in kisses when his brother was distracted. She had no business dallying with him, especially since his touch made her want to do things with him that she'd heard the girls in the brothel discuss. Not that she had any experience with such activities, but as the week went on, she found herself looking forward to his visits so she could imagine them.

He returned every day as promised, and as her shoulder and neck loosened under his touch, so did the binds around her heart. She admired how he interacted with his brother and the tenderness there. He would be a great husband and father, and she sensed his desire to grow into the man he thought he should be. It was different from what she'd felt before, the need to avoid the entrapment of marriage and family, and she was proud of him even though she mourned that it would be with some other woman.

She also felt his curiosity about her, which was both flattering and terrifying. He continued to ask about her past, and she kept evading his questions without lying. Let him keep his illusions about her so he'd remember her well when she left and he settled down with one of the noble ladies of the village. At least one of them would have a happy ending.

For as her days were filled with happiness and progress, a living nightmare consumed her evenings. On Monday, she'd felt the merest brush of the man who sought her. Then on Tuesday, he had been behind her, still questing. She'd kept her head down, but just before she'd turned the corner, there had been something of a triumphant stab, and she'd almost run the whole way back to the boarding house.

She wasn't sure if she could trust Mrs. Culvert. What if the man who sought her offered more money to the boarding house mistress than what she extorted from Pauline? It seemed like every day she found some reason to charge Pauline something, and Pauline couldn't argue. She counted down the days until Friday, when the duke was to pay her.

Finally, Friday came. Pauline helped the professor put the finishing touches on the aether isolater, which had been constructed from the various parts he'd extracted from the boxes.

"It looks complicated," she said. It had three copper and three glass globes connected with tubing.

"I suspect that the final design will be more simple," the professor said. "Probably just two globes. But what's the fun in that?"

His grin reminded her he was only twenty, and boys did like their toys. Thankfully this one preferred mechanical ones to female. With his blue eyes and the potential to grow into a handsome man like the duke, he would attract the right young woman someday.

She envied his privileged childhood, where he could play with his own and others' resources like that. She turned away to see Christopher watching them from the door.

"Is it done?" he asked.

"Yes!" The professor gestured to the apparatus. "Perhaps I shall be the first to tease into visible existence this strange substance called aether."

Christopher joined them at the table by the window. "What does it do?"

Edward pointed to his calculations. "It's going to create a vacuum to eliminate anything in the glass globes except the light and the substance that carries it, aether. Then I'm going to apply different frequencies to the globes to see which one shows something. I suspect it will be the one in the middle. It should be isolated from the other two with the rubber gaskets—very hard to get, by the way—but I suspect the layers of frequencies will cause it to appear, like ripples in water reveal the shape of the substance. This is the most complete set of tuning forks in England."

Christopher stood by Pauline, and she felt his warm presence with every cell of her body on her right side, like he was the tuning fork and she the instrument set to his frequency. She resisted the urge to lean into him. He emanated the simultaneous need to see Edward's success and concern that he would no longer have an excuse to come to the department.

The professor started the burners under the globes. Then, when they were heated, he poured cool water over the copper ones. "This creates the vacuum," he explained.

He plucked three tuning forks from the leather case on the floor. "According to my calculations, these have the greatest chance of working."

He struck the first and held it to the globe on the left. Nothing happened. Then he did the same with the one on the right. Again, nothing. When he held the third one to the copper globe attached to the glass globe at the center, Pauline squinted at what looked like a little cloud.

"Is that it?" she whispered.

Edward peered into the globe. "Yes, that's it," he murmured. It dissipated in a few seconds, but the professor turned to her with the biggest smile she'd seen on him yet.

"This is a historical moment—we've isolated it."

They stood and looked at the now-empty globe. "Can you do it again?" Pauline asked. "That's the point of experimentation, right?"

"Yes, now I'm going to work with different frequencies to see if I can get a stronger isolation and simplify the design to just one specific frequency. The math shouldn't be too difficult. Thank you for your help."

"You're welcome." She turned to Christopher. "I suppose I'll return to my regular position, then." The words stuck in her throat, but she forced them out. "And I suppose we should discuss payment, Your Grace."

"I suppose we should. And Mother said to tell you to come for lunch. She would like to thank you for your work with Edward, too."

Pauline nodded but couldn't say anything. She felt the

professor's joy in his scientific triumph and his need to progress with it. It would help to heal his heart, so he no longer needed her. She also felt the duke's desire for her, but asking for money reminded her where she came from and that nothing could ever be between them. She couldn't return to the site of their kiss.

"Please give your mother my regrets, but I cannot."

"Come now. It's almost lunchtime, and your fee is at the house. I forgot to bring it with me."

Pauline could catch the three fifteen train to Newcastle if she got the money. "All right, I'll come."

She felt a hand on her shoulder and turned to see the professor behind her.

"I hope you'll come to the ball tomorrow," he said. "In case, you know. It will help to have you there."

That anxiety could replace triumph so quickly reminded her that his heart was not completely healed.

"I'll ponder it, but girls like me don't have anything to wear to such things. I'm sure you'll be fine."

Uncertainty flickered over his face. "If you say so."

Pauline prided herself on seeing things through. She would have to seriously consider delaying her departure, if only to protect the professor from a breakdown should Lily Cavender show up at the ball.

8

____

D *uke of Waltham's Townhouse, 11 July 1862*

WHEN HORACE OPENED THE DOOR, his eyebrows raised in surprise. Pauline allowed her expression to mimic his.

"Miss Danahue, I am surprised to see you've returned."

"What's the fun in life if I can't keep men on their toes?" she asked and immediately regretted her flippancy.

"Indeed." He stepped aside to allow her to enter. "Where are the duke and Professor Bailey?"

"Finishing up something at the university. Apparently the duchess is expecting me."

He didn't argue, only gestured for her to follow him. Since it was her second visit and Pauline wasn't quite as nervous as the first time, she looked around, but she found herself not as curious as she thought she'd be. She got a flash of memory of having been somewhere grander, but where everything was taller. She couldn't chase the wisp, however, because they entered the dining room, where the duchess sat at the head of the table. When Pauline entered, the duchess looked up from...

A newspaper!

Pauline's smile went from forced to genuine. "Good afternoon, Your Grace," she said.

"Good afternoon, Miss Danahue." The duchess gestured for her to sit at the only other set place.

Pauline blinked but didn't question the lack of place settings. She settled in the chair and tried not to show how she felt shabby among the antiques and expensively patterned damask wallpaper.

"Christopher is taking Edward to lunch at the public house," the duchess said. "So it's just you and me."

"I see." Now Pauline felt trapped.

"Hopefully you don't mind keeping an old lady company for lunch."

"Not at all, Your Grace." But she stayed on high alert. A duchess didn't invite a mere secretary to dine with her.

"Good." The duchess rang a bell, and a footman appeared. "The first course, please."

Pauline tried not to allow the newspaper to distract her attention. She'd not been able to keep up with her mother's murder case—fascinating to the police and the press since it was the first of a string of similar ones—and her anxiety rose like the thermometer had that morning.

"Would you like to see the paper, dear?" The duchess scooted it toward Pauline. "I know it's not looked upon kindly for women to be interested in such things, but when one has investments across the empire, it helps to keep abreast of current events."

"Thank you." Pauline wrenched her eyes away from the first sentence of the article—

Inspector Davidson has gone into the country to pursue a promising lead...

Perhaps the duchess would allow her to read it later, but she felt rude doing so and ignoring her hostess in the moment. She set the paper aside.

"If you wouldn't mind, I'd like to look at it later. I wasn't able to get one this morning, and I agree with you about staying informed. The world is a big place."

The duchess nodded as though Pauline had passed some test. "Yes, and there is no excuse for being ignorant of potential danger. Like those poor girls in London."

"I doubt they were expecting to be murdered," Pauline said. She knew her mother certainly hadn't, and she felt piqued at the implication that somehow it had been her fault.

"No, but after the first one, you'd think there would have been more precautions taken."

Pauline shrugged. "I wouldn't know." Because she had fled. Guilt pricked her—had her leaving put other girls in danger because she hadn't stayed to help the police? But she couldn't have stayed, else she would have ended up like her mother.

The footman brought out a tray with two bowls of soup. Pauline was relieved to see hers was a cold tomato soup—it was too hot to put warm liquid in her stomach—and she noticed the duchess's was steaming. She waited for the duchess to take the first bite and hoped her hostess didn't notice her stomach growling at the smell. Once the duchess took a dainty spoonful, Pauline lifted her own spoon to her lips.

The soup's delicate spices warmed Pauline, but in a nice way.

"How is Edward progressing?" the duchess asked. "He seemed very excited last night when he arrived here."

"He isolated a small bit of aether this morning, so he has accomplished what the department hoped."

"Oh, that's grand news!" The duchess pushed her half-finished soup away.

Pauline looked down at her empty bowl. She reminded herself she needed to eat at a ladylike pace, not inhale her food.

The footman cleared the bowls, and another one brought out two plates, these with roast beef, green beans, and roasted potatoes. The first entered with a gravy boat.

"I apologize for the simplicity of our fare today." The duchess gestured for Pauline to help herself to the gravy. "Our main cook is at the country house preparing for tomorrow's ball. Will you be coming, dear?"

"Professor Bailey just invited me this morning. I'm afraid I don't have anything to wear." *Eat slowly. This is the best beef you've had in, well, ever.*

"Oh, of course. How stupid of us." The duchess shrugged. "Then let me give you a gift. You'll need a dress made or altered in a rush, and I know the university doesn't pay you that well, so how would a hundred pounds do?"

Pauline almost dropped the gravy boat. A brown drop escaped on to the white tablecloth. "A hundred pounds? That's very generous, Your Grace."

"And of course you don't have to use it for a dress if you have something else you'd prefer to do with the money."

Pauline swallowed and forced herself to look into the duchess's eyes. "Excuse me?"

"I do hope you'll come to the ball because I know it would mean the world to Edward, and I'm sure Christopher would be happy for you to be there, too. He seems quite taken with you. But I'm torn."

"How so?" She ignored the little thrill in her stomach at the duchess's revelation that Christopher felt something for her.

"Well, I know it would be reassuring for Edward, but I don't want Christopher to be distracted from his purpose of finding a wife."

Pauline's cheeks heated. Of course. That was why she was here. Not for the duchess to express any appreciation for what she'd done for the professor, but rather to warn her away from Christopher. But the haunted look in the professor's eyes came back to her.

"If I can be frank," she said.

The duchess nodded. "Please. That's what this lunch is for, for us to get to know each other better."

"I know I am not a suitable match for the duke." She had to breathe deeply against the pain that clawed from her heart to her throat at saying it. "But the professor is very anxious that the woman who broke his heart will appear and try to reconcile with him. He is still inexperienced with regard to matters of the heart, after all, and he asked me to be there."

"Then the decision is yours. I'm sure you will do the right thing." But her tone said otherwise.

The duchess kept the topics light for the rest of the meal, which dragged on for Pauline. Finally the duchess drew up a note for a hundred pounds and five shillings. Pauline accepted it and the newspaper and fled—this time out the front door.

CHRISTOPHER CAUGHT sight of Pauline as she walked out the front door of the townhouse. He burned to know what his mother had discovered, but the look on Pauline's face stopped him from merely greeting her and going in. He waited for her at the bottom of the townhouse steps.

"Oh, Your Grace," she said. The dismay disappeared from her face to be replaced by her typical friendly expression.

"How was lunch?" he asked.

The door of the next townhouse opened, and Christopher glanced up to see the back of the man, who spoke with someone inside. When he returned his attention to Pauline, he saw her face had gone ashen. He instinctively stepped between her and his neighbor.

"What's wrong?" he asked.

She tugged his sleeve and ducked into the alley between the two houses. She ran faster than he expected on her heeled boots and with her heavy skirts, but he kept up with her. When they reached the back alley, he opened the garden gate. Finally she stopped, leaned against the fig tree and panted.

"What was that all about?"

She sank onto the bench and looked at the ground between them. "I shouldn't stay here, but I need to rest a minute."

He sat beside her and took her hands. With a small squeeze, he said, "Look at me. You can tell me what's going on. If you feel you're in danger, I want to know so I can protect you."

She complied, and the line between her brows appeared. "Danger? Who said anything about danger?"

"Pauline, I need you to tell me everything."

She pulled away and stood. "I have nothing to say, Your Grace. You know there can't be anything between us except friendship, and I can't bear just that."

He rose and put his hands on her shoulders. They felt familiar after he'd worked on them all week, and his thumbs found the tight spots just inside her shoulder blades. He massaged them and said, "Who says there can't be? I'm a duke. I can do what I want."

She tensed and turned to him. "But you can't. Your mother made that quite clear. A duke can't marry the daughter of a—" She covered her mouth.

"The daughter of a what?" He raised her chin and made her look at him. "Tell me, Pauline. Who were your parents?"

9

D*uke of Waltham's Townhouse, 11 July 1862*

PAULINE'S LUNGS strained against her ribs, but the exertion from her mad dash down the alley had passed. Now the struggle was internal. She could tell him, take his mother's money, and use it to flee the country. A hundred pounds plus what she had should be enough for a passage to the United States. Although the Americans fought among themselves, she was sure she could get lost in the vastness she'd heard about.

Her body softened against his in spite of her resolve to stay as far away from temptation as possible. She could lie to him and stay with him, but then they both would be ruined when her secret inevitably came to light.

Plus, *he* was near. She felt him, but Christopher had blocked her view before she got more than a quick impression of dark hair—the same that had waved above the mask he'd worn when he'd visited and then killed her mother.

No, it was better to come clean and have him cast her aside before she fell more in love with him.

"I'm not who you think I am, Your Grace."

He took her hands again. "Why this formality? You know I don't care for it."

She looked aside, and he kissed her cheekbone. She closed her eyes against the ripping sensation in her chest and forced out the words, "My mother was a prostitute in a brothel in the northern end of London. She serviced the nobility, but she was still a whore. I don't know who my father was. So you see, Your Grace, I cannot be your wife, and I will not follow in my mother's ill-fated footsteps and be your lover."

"I see." He didn't release her hands, but he'd gone still. "I suspected as much, but..."

"But?" She looked up at him, but her tears distorted his face. All she could see with certainty was the brilliant blue of his eyes. "And you *suspected*?"

She didn't know whether to laugh or continue to cry, her feelings were so mixed up. He knew, or thought she might be low-born? Then what had he been doing all this time? She thought he had some affection for her, but was he just using her with no intention to marry her?

On the other hand, she was the one who wanted to do sinful things with him, and although she thought he felt the same, maybe he didn't. Maybe he was just being kind and caring because that was who he was.

Her head spun with the thoughts that whirled around inside, back and forth, and he steadied her.

"You're in danger," he said. "An Inspector Davidson from London came to visit me. He had a picture that may have been you, but it wasn't very good."

She tried to draw her hands back, but he held her.

"Listen to me, Pauline. Someone has been killing dark-haired prostitutes in London. The inspector thinks you're next."

Pauline nodded. "He killed my mother. I saw him, but not his face." She lowered her voice. "I think it's your neighbor."

Now he frowned. "Why? You said you didn't see his face."

She couldn't explain lest he think her mad. "I saw enough."

He didn't ask for any further explanation. "Then we need to go to Inspector Davidson. He can sort it out. Meanwhile, you need to stay with me. I'll keep you safe."

"No, I need to flee. Nowhere is safe from him." She needed to escape before he uncovered or stumbled upon all her secrets.

"But what about Edward? He's counting on you to be there tomorrow. And if you abandon him precipitously, it could cause another breakdown."

Poor Edward. Christopher was right—her leaving at this point would be a different kind of blow, but still as harsh as a romantic rejection. If only she felt secure that the murderer, who drew closer with each day, wouldn't find her.

And if Mrs. Culvert somehow found out about her financial windfall...

"You could stay here," Christopher told her. "I'll tell Horace to have the maid prepare a room for you. Or, even better, I'll take you out to the country house."

She took one hand from his and wiped her eyes. He used his free hand to pull a handkerchief from his pocket and give it to her. She thrilled that he wanted to protect her and his brother, but he was a man, and they had such instincts. She wanted him to say *he* was counting on her to be at the ball rather than hiding behind the professor, but she had just told him anything between them would be impossible. Regardless, she could hide at the country house and put off leaving for a day for Edward.

"Fine, I will stay."

"Good."

Pauline laughed at the ridiculously feminine thought that popped into her head.

Now he did look at her like she deserved a one-way ticket to Bedlam. "What's so funny?"

"I need a dress for the ball."

"CHRISTOPHER, I didn't hear you come in, or did you sneak through the garden?"

He tensed at his mother's tone but didn't let go of Pauline's hand. He wasn't sure what his mother had said to her, only that she, too, suspected that Pauline had hidden her background.

"Mother, you remember Miss Danahue." They walked into the parlor, where his mother reclined on the chaise, a cool cloth across her brow and eyes. A half-empty cup of tea and the laudanum bottle sat on the table in front of her.

"Of course, dear. She left here less than half an hour ago. My body might be failing, but there's nothing wrong with my mind."

He reminded himself that he was the duke, and he didn't need to ask her permission for anything. "Miss Danahue is in danger. I'm going to send her to the country house, but she needs a dress for the ball. Which modiste in town do you recommend?"

The duchess lifted the cloth from her eyes, and she frowned. "Do you have some sort of arrangement with her that I'm not aware of? I invited her to lunch to remind her of her proper place in your marital strategy, not to give my blessing on whatever activities you might be engaged in."

Christopher wanted to confront her with the suggestion she'd made that morning, but he sensed they all played a part in a drama of how these things were supposed to go. He was tired of doing what he was supposed to, but before he could say anything, Pauline jerked her hand from his.

"We don't have any sort of arrangement, Your Grace. Nor have I been engaged in any *activities* with him."

"Good. Use Madame LaFleur on the square. She has the best assortment of ready-made gowns, and I gave you enough money to pay her to put your alterations at the top of her priority list." She replaced the compress and waved them away. "Now leave me. You're tiring me."

Christopher could tell she wasn't pleased, but he was done with people telling him what he ought to do. "Mother, Pauline is my guest. Please speak to her with respect."

"Pauline?" The duchess peeked from beneath her eye cloth. "Are you on such intimate terms with her?"

He wanted to say, "Not yet," but the look on Pauline's face stopped him. "No, she is a friend in trouble, and she has greatly helped Edward."

"Then I apologize for my harsh words."

Christopher wanted to say more, but Pauline pulled on his hand.

"Rest well, Your Grace," she said.

He followed her into the hall.

"Thank you, but that wasn't necessary," she told him.

"What wasn't?"

"Having her apologize."

His sense of victory deflated. "What would you have me do?"

"I don't know." She rubbed her eyes. "Everything has gone topsy-turvy. Allow me to go to the modiste, and I'll meet you at the university at five o'clock."

"But how do I know you'll be safe?"

"The murderer won't strike during the day in a public place. He likes to lure his victims aside and toy with them."

"Fine," he said and drew her into his arms. "But be careful."

She had to look up at him, so he pressed his lips to hers. He trailed a hand down her back and cupped her...bustle. He kept himself from sighing and focused on the feel of her mouth, her small tongue exploring his.

The sound of Horace clearing his throat broke them apart. The butler raised his eyebrows at them and disappeared into the back hall.

"I must go," Pauline said. She broke away and paused by the front door. Then she did something strange. She closed her eyes, and the line between her brows reappeared. Then her shoulders slumped as though she released tension she'd been holding, and she slipped out.

What was that about?

But he didn't have time to wonder. He needed to talk to Inspector Davidson. He was reluctant to hand Pauline over to the inspector, but if it would keep her safe...

He shook his head. At the very least, if his neighbor was the prostitute murderer, he needed to know and have the man put behind bars before he hurt anyone else.

WALTHAM MANOR, *12 July 1862*

PAULINE FLOATED IN A DREAM. She'd woken on a thick mattress in soft sheets, had been attended to by a maid—thankfully not one she knew from the boarding house—and had eaten two regular meals and drunk strong tea with the indulgence of real cream and sugar.

Something tickled the back of her mind—that she'd lived like this before in the distant past.

After lunch, she'd rested, and then the same maid had helped her into her ball gown and done her hair in the latest style of being piled on her head, but not too high. She lacked jewelry, but a courier had delivered a box containing two diamond and pearl earbobs and a pearl choker.

To say thank you, the card read. The maid didn't say anything, only complimented the jewelry, but Pauline could feel her desire to know if the thank you note was a cover-up for a gift to the duke's mistress.

Christopher had not accompanied his mother, and he'd been absent all day. Pauline told herself her disappointment was stupid—she couldn't expect the duke to play house with her when he had important business to attend to. The duchess had arrived the previous evening but had taken her meals in her chambers. Pauline guessed she was resting up for the ball. At least that was what she told herself, but she also suspected the duchess avoided her.

Idleness had never sat well with her, and the guests wouldn't start to arrive for another hour, so Pauline went downstairs to see if she could help in any way. Although it was still bright early evening, the curtains were drawn, and the candles in sconces were lit. She breathed in the scent of fresh cut flowers, their heady fragrance mingled with the green sharpness of the cut leaves and stems. Everything was in pastels and white, hinting at the purpose of the ball as a pre-wedding where the duke would choose his wife.

Pauline wore a gown of dark rose that had flattered her coloring in the shop, but amid all the delicate colors, she felt she stood out like a sore.

"Miss Danahue?"

The young man who approached her wore a simple suit, nice but inexpensive. His freckles told of outdoor work.

"Can I help you?"

He held out his hand. "I'm Inspector Davidson. The duke said I might speak to you before the ball."

"Oh, did he?" She didn't know whether to be angrier at this man approaching her without an introduction or chaperon or at Christopher for setting her up. She crossed her arms against the chill that occurred when she recognized his name from the newspaper article.

After an awkward moment with him stretched out like a scarecrow, he drew his hand back. "I'm sorry to offend you, but I must ask you some questions."

"About the murders."

"And other things."

A group of footmen came through carrying yet more flowers. Pauline gestured for the inspector to follow her into the dining room, where chafing dishes stood empty, but savory and yeasty smells wafted from the kitchen.

"We should be undisturbed here, but there are enough ears nearby," she said. "What do you need to ask me?"

"Where are you from?" he asked. She frowned, and his ears turned pink under his sandy hair. "I mean, where did you grow up?"

"London," she said. She sensed his desire to get the truth from her without leading her to certain answers, but there was also the need to prove something.

That piqued her curiosity. He was definitely young—barely older than Edward—so how was he already an inspector?

"And were you born there?"

Now she felt herself reddening. "I honestly don't know."

"You don't know where you were born?" He looked up from the little pad of paper in his hand.

"No, I don't. My mother never told me, only that we were English, and that was all anyone needed to know."

But why hadn't her mother given her more details? Because she knew exactly what to say to satisfy Pauline's curiosity without revealing too much.

Pauline had never thought of it before—she'd thought it was to keep her safe in the brothel, but was there more?

"And where was your mother from?"

Pauline again found herself without an answer. "I don't know."

Even if she was the daughter of a whore, she should know where her mother was from and where she had been born.

Had she allowed herself to buy into the belief others had of women in her position, that they didn't deserve normal lives including a sense of personal history? Or had she decided not to ask for information that would tie her to a past she wanted to escape?

The inspector pressed on, "Do you know if your mother was married before she took up her profession?"

Pauline opened her mouth to say no, but something stopped her. It seemed there had been a life before the brothel, but if there had been, she had been very young. "I... I don't know. I don't remember. If she was, she didn't say."

He nodded and flipped to a new page. "Thank you."

A chill poured through Pauline's blood vessels at his desire to know more about her because he felt he was close. To what? Would she be trapped here with the man who killed her mother? Was the inspector going to give her up to him to see if she'd end up dead?

"What do you know of the killer?" he asked.

She decided she'd had enough of the inspector. If he was going to ask her odd questions without giving her any answers, then she wouldn't make it easy for him.

Not that she could.

"I never saw his face—he always wore a mask or cloak with a deep hood. There was speculation he was of the gentry."

"Did you see anything? Height? Build?"

"He was always covered. I only know that he had lots of wavy dark hair."

Davidson shut his notebook with a snap. "You do realize you are our only eyewitness to these crimes. Can you give me any other information?"

She wanted to tell him about her sensation of being stalked and her suspicion that the duke's neighbor was the killer, but she didn't have anything solid on which to base her accusation. And she knew what she risked by accusing a nobleman of a crime—such acts typically did not go well for a young commoner, especially a female.

The inspector was holding something back. Perhaps if she had that information, she could reveal her hunch.

"Who else has been looking for me?" she demanded. "If I'm in danger, as you and the duke seem to think, I have a right to know."

"I agree." He bowed slightly. "I'll get back with you shortly. Enjoy the ball."

He walked out of the dining room, leaving her astonished. She went to follow him but bumped into a footman. She smiled, but the cold look in his eyes froze the expression on her face, and she stepped back from the wave of destructive desire that emanated from him.

The prostitutes had taught her tricks of cosmetics that could subtly alter a person's appearance even to changing the shape of their facial features, and her heart fluttered when she saw underneath his disguise and imagined the shape of his hair were it not to be slicked back.

It was the Duke's neighbor.

10

———

W*altham Manor, 12 July 1862*

Pauline's mother's voice came back to her—*If a man threatens you, it's better for him to be in front of you because with a swift movement, you can disable him where it hurts.*

Right, although she was dressed as a proper miss, she wasn't one, and she wasn't going to swoon, faint, or give up her life to an insane man. Hopefully her many layers of skirt would allow her one good, swift—

The door from the kitchen opened, and Horace appeared with two footmen, who carried a large crystal bowl of—what else?—pastel pink punch between them. The butler looked at Pauline and the footman with his customary raised eyebrows.

"Miss Danahue, have you lost your way?" he asked.

"Yes, and I was just directing her to the ballroom," the footman said. "It's that way, Miss, across the front hall." And in a lower voice, "We'll finish this later." He disappeared into the kitchen.

Pauline ran into Horace in the front hall. He looked down at her with a haughty expression.

"I suggest that you make up your mind between dallying with the duke and doing so with men of your station. His Grace will not be amused to find out his mistress has been seen with another."

"I'm not his mistress, and how dare you? You know there was nothing going on aside from the fact that I think that man wants to kill me."

"If you continue to make disruptive accusations, I shall have you removed."

Frustrated tears tried to escape her eyes, but she refused to let them. "I'm going to tell His Grace."

"Go ahead. The duchess is still in charge here." With that, he brushed past her.

Pauline steadied herself on the banister of the grand staircase that led to the second floor. Perhaps she should remove herself, take the rest of the duchess's money and flee to the coast to catch a ship to...

Well, somewhere other than here.

She gathered her skirts and had just stepped on the first stair when she heard the professor's voice behind her.

"Miss Danahue! There you are. I was afraid you wouldn't come."

She forced a smile that turned genuine when she turned to him. "You look well." And he did. He had color in his cheeks. The sad expression that had haunted him when she'd first met him—and which had recurred after he'd gotten the twit's note —was gone. Now he looked like a young scientist proud of his accomplishments.

"Have you seen the steamcarts outside? There are only a few, but they're marvelous." He tugged at her hand. "Come on! I know the perfect window to watch them from without being seen."

"Edward, don't monopolize Miss Danahue's time." The duke descended the stairs. He looked so handsome in his formal wear.

Pauline's heart gave a little thud that had nothing to do with her scare. She could admire him and enjoy the reciprocal desire in his eyes as he looked her over, but he was not for her. No matter what, she had to remember that and leave as soon as she could slip away.

CHRISTOPHER DISMISSED his valet and looked at himself in the mirror. He wore his best suit, and his valet had tied his cravat in a splendid knot. He should look—feel—excited, but he had more of a sense of going to his own funeral.

He knew Pauline was somewhere in the house. He'd wanted to see her for lunch, at least, but he'd been busy planning what to do with Inspector Davidson. He believed Pauline that his neighbor could be the murderer, but as the inspector had said, he couldn't arrest the man without more solid proof than a woman's hunch and a description of his hair. Davidson had reached out to some of his colleagues in London to gather more information about the lead, but it would take time for them to question people and respond. Time Christopher didn't have, for he sensed Pauline would say her goodbyes to Edward at the ball and disappear. He couldn't stand the thought of her leaving.

Not that he knew what he'd do if he convinced her to stay— they still couldn't marry.

Or could they? He was tired of playing by society's rules. He would figure out a way to make her his wife. There had to be something... And if he couldn't figure it out, surely Edward with his prodigious intellect could.

For the first time that day, he smiled. He and Edward could solve this little problem of Pauline's parentage. Now all he had to do was find her.

Thankfully, she was at the bottom of the grand stairwell talking to Edward. A woman of good breeding would know to be somewhere else so she could make an entrance, but he shoved the thought to the back of his mind.

Christopher knew Pauline would be stunning in her gown, but knowing and being prepared to see her were two different things. She stood out against the crystal and pastel decorations in a dress that wasn't quite pink and wasn't quite red. She looked like the only vibrant thing in the house amid the duchess's washed-out color scheme.

"You look lovely," he said and took her hands.

"Thank you." She looked into his eyes. "And you're very handsome."

"I have something to ask you before the firsts guests arrive." But he stopped. The little line was between her brows. "What's wrong?"

She leaned in to allow Edward to pass her at the bottom of the stairs. Christopher knew he went to watch the guests' arrival from an upstairs bedroom so as not to be caught up in the boring ritual of greeting, which was fine with him.

"Your neighbor is here," she said once Edward had disappeared upstairs. She turned her wide brown eyes to him, and he wanted to wipe away the tears that threatened.

"Where?" He wanted to kill the man for frightening her and for his murderous intent.

"He's disguised as one of the footmen, and it's so good that you may not recognize him. How many extra people did you and your mother hire for this affair?"

"At least a dozen. You'll have to point him out to me and Inspector Davidson, then. Have you met the inspector?"

"Yes." Now her cheekbones stood out as her jaw clenched. "He cornered me and asked me several interesting questions. What do you know of him? What does he want with me?"

Christopher rubbed the back of his head. "I don't know exactly what, only that he asked for two invitations, one for himself and one for a guest who wouldn't be accompanying him romantically. He assured me they would pass my mother's muster."

A maid approached them. "Your Grace, the duchess says it's almost time to be in position to welcome the guests, and she requires your assistance."

"Come with me," he told Pauline.

"I'm not sure your mother will welcome my presence."

"She will have to." And he meant it. Her hand on his arm gave him a new strength of resolve. It was more than her being in danger; it was the fact that she knew and hadn't run in spite of having the resources to do so because of her concern for Edward. Silly Edward. He'd likely never realize what a sacrifice she made to help him heal from his neurosis.

"In all honesty, I might be more afraid of the duchess than the murderer," she murmured.

He paused in front of a large display of flowers that had been set up around a fountain that looked like stone, but which was obviously paste and wood. The ballroom stood empty, the maid having disappeared, presumably back to the duchess. The doors to the garden terrace stood open to allow in the cool breeze. Christopher turned Pauline so she faced him and took both her hands.

"Pauline Danahue, I have an important question for you."

Her eyes widened, and the wariness in them would have broken his heart had it not been so full of another emotion.

"I love you," he said. "You're beautiful and graceful, but

inside, there's a core of steel that I've not found in any of the noble women of my acquaintance. You have a wonderful sense of humor, and you know how to keep us Bailey men in line. I can't think of a more perfect duchess than you."

Instead of happiness, the line appeared between her brows. "While I appreciate your sentiment—and I love you, too—I fit all the requirements you laid out, but not one of import. I am of low birth, and I will not ruin your place in society. I also don't want that for my children, the whispers that will follow them through their schooling."

"And there's another reason," a voice said from behind the installation. An unfamiliar footman appeared brandishing a gun. "You will not leave this ballroom alive."

PAULINE HAD BEEN SO CAUGHT up trying to decipher Christopher's needs, determine what was protectiveness and what was true desire to marry her that she had missed the footman. He now emanated the desire to destroy her. She'd known what he wanted to do to her, but why? If there was one thing she'd learned from all those hours helping Edward, it was that there was always a cause to each effect. Now that she was caught, she needed to convince the footman it wasn't worthwhile for him to murder a duke. Perhaps finding out why this madman had pursued her could save Christopher.

"What do you want with me?" she asked. "I haven't done anything to you, and I am no one of import."

"That's what you think," he said. "My brother did a clever thing, hiding you and your mother away. It took me years to find her."

"Your brother?" Pauline's heartbeat galloped in her chest, an echo to a distant memory of a late-night coach ride. "You mean my father?"

"Yes, he paid that whorehouse in London to keep you and your mother hidden. She was a clever woman. It took me months to determine who she was."

"I..." Pauline swallowed against the competing waves of desire, Christopher's to protect and the madman's to destroy. And hers to escape but also save Christopher. "I was not aware." It seemed so unfair—she was of noble birth, or she must be. The memories of the ice and seeing a grand house from a small position could mean she'd had a privileged early childhood. At the very least she wasn't the daughter of a whore. She added hope, however faint, to the raging stew of feelings she juggled from within and without. "Why not just allow me to go, then, warn me away?" She blinked back tears. "I would have lived a happy, or at least mildly contented life knowing I hadn't ruined his."

Christopher squeezed the one hand he held onto. "But I wouldn't have."

The madman held the revolver steady. "Your mother was a stubborn woman, and I suspect you are, too. I am truly sorry your paramour won't survive, but now he knows too much."

Christopher tried to pull Pauline behind him, but she refused. She'd been running and hiding long enough, and it hadn't done her any good. She would take care of this.

"Let him go," she put all her feminine influence behind the words. "There is no reason to murder him. You still haven't told us who I am, and I assure you, I do not know."

"But he will find out soon, and he is now a witness. Now move toward the terrace, please. We'll finish this in the woods."

11

W *altham Manor, 12 July 1862*

PAULINE TRIED to edge away from Christopher toward the flower and fountain installation. If she could separate from him enough, he could possibly escape when the man—her uncle?—shot her. She pushed back against his hand so he wouldn't move.

"Since you're going to kill me anyway, at least give me the satisfaction of knowing who I am," she said.

The man hesitated, and Pauline sensed his need to keep this secret to the end, but also a strange sense of regret. "Very well," he said. "You are Lisette deMarco, the daughter of a Spanish nobleman and an English Marchioness."

If Pauline hadn't been looking at her own death, she would have jumped for joy. "And my father is dead. Did you kill him?"

The false footman shrugged. "I will not claim responsibility, although I did not mourn his passing."

Now Christopher spoke, and his tone echoed his own sadness. He needed for her to be safe, but he also emanated hopelessness, frustration, and the desire to change the past. "Pauline, you cannot reason with him. I know how this works. The will was worded in such a way that this man cannot inherit the family fortune if his brother's child is still alive, and once you marry, it will all go to your husband."

"Very clever, *Señor*."

With the installation at her back, Pauline used the scent of the flowers and the running water to dampen her sensation of the two men's desires. Now she caught the feeling of a third—the need of Inspector Davidson to prove himself as a competent policeman. But where was he? If she could keep the gunman talking, she could figure out what to do.

"And what is your name...Uncle?"

"I am Carlos DeMarco. I would say at your service, as they do in books, but I am most definitely not. And time grows short. Your guests will be arriving soon." He gestured for them to move together.

"If you have any mercy in you, do not kill her," Christopher said. "My brother is not of sound mind, and to lose us both may unsettle him permanently."

"There is no mercy shown to younger siblings," Carlos told him with a sneer. "As I well know. As you said, I am not a reasonable man and will not be dissuaded."

Davidson's desire changed from proving himself to protecting Pauline. She needed to ensure DeMarco didn't see the detective before Davidson could intervene. A quick glance showed her where one of the wooden supports protruded, so she grasped it and pulled. The entire flower structure toppled down on her, pressing her to the ground beneath it. Two shots rang out, and someone groaned. One of the clay pots fell on Pauline's head, and she blacked out.

CHRISTOPHER HEARD THE SHOTS, but he had no care for himself. Pauline was under the ridiculous bouquet-fountain thing his mother had ordered. He dove in, tearing the plants apart and tossing aside pots until he found her, pale and unconscious. His heart stopped with a sharp pang like he'd been the one shot.

Davidson pulled him away from Pauline and checked her pulse. "She's alive," he said. "It looks like one of the pots fell atop her."

Christopher picked her up and brought her to a couch behind a screen of potted plants. He had to step over the body of Carlos DeMarco to reach it and was careful not to get the man's blood on his shoes.

"Good shot," Christopher said once he'd laid Pauline down and ordered one of the servants to bring a cool compress for her head.

"Thanks." Davidson looked back at the prone body of the Spaniard. "The girl has a good head on her shoulders. You'll do well not to let her go."

"Believe me," Christopher told him. "I have no intention to." But her courage and willingness to sacrifice herself—she couldn't have known how heavy the arrangement was—only made him more ashamed of what he'd done to bring her into his life. He would have to find a time to tell her about the trick he'd played on Edward, but now he needed to know she was all right. He brushed a hand along Pauline's cheek, and her eyelids fluttered open.

"Christopher?" she asked. "You're alive!" She struggled to sit, but he pressed her back.

"Lie still," he ordered, then added, "my love. I've sent a maid for something for your head. And for the doctor."

Her eyebrows pressed the line into visibility between them. "What happened?"

"You are an exceedingly clever young woman," Davidson said. "You managed to distract him long enough for me to get a shot off and stop him."

"So he's...?"

"Dead," Christopher said. "And no one else is hurt. You saved us with your quick thinking."

"Yes," Davidson told her with words that chilled Christopher. "I think he'd seen me out of the corner of his eye, so your distraction was well-timed."

"But the ball! The flowers!" She looked down. "And my poor dress."

"We'll call off the ball." Christopher squeezed her hand. "And you've never looked lovelier."

"What is this nonsense about calling off the ball?" the duchess asked. "And what is this mess? And why is that man bleeding all over the floor?"

"Let me sit," Pauline said. Christopher helped her to a semi-reclined position. She leaned back onto a cool compress, which she positioned to fit under the spot where the pot had hit her. She could barely see the ballroom through the plants, but she couldn't help but look for her uncle's body.

The duchess clomped over, making a ridiculous amount of noise for a frail woman with a cane.

"What is the meaning of this?" she asked.

"I am sorry, Duchess," another man said, his voice accented with a rhythm that prompted a strange wave of homesickness in Pauline. She contained her curiosity and waited for him to follow the older woman into their little room within a room.

"You should be. And who are you?" The duchess's hands trembled on her cane. Christopher reached to help her sit, but she batted his hand away. "Don't go treating me like an invalid,

Christopher Joseph Bailey. I demand an explanation at once! The guests are about to arrive, and we can't have foreigners shot in the ballroom."

The slight twitch of the duchess's lips told Pauline she appreciated the ridiculousness of the situation. She winked —*winked!*—at Pauline. But Pauline couldn't respond because she stared at the older gentleman who shook hands with Inspector Davidson.

"So it's done, then?" he asked. "I am truly sorry, Your Graces. I tried to keep this tragedy from happening, but I needed to see if this was, indeed, my great niece first." He took Pauline in with his dark eyes. "And I can say she is the image of her mother at that age, although I see a bit of my nephew in her as well."

A snippet of a memory floated into Pauline's mind. He had handed her mother into a coach where Pauline waited.

"The situation will be temporary," he'd said. *"You will only have to stay until I can convince the authorities to put Carlos away and settle his debts. Then it will be safe for you to return."*

"You sent us away," she said. "You're the reason we went to London."

He nodded. "Do you remember where you were born and spent your early childhood? The house with the wide green lawn and the fountain with the mermaid?"

Pauline's memories floated to the surface like bubbles in a murky pond. "I think so. But what happened to my father?"

"He had a tragic riding accident, leaving a grieving widow and small daughter. Yes, your mother came to her people, but then Carlos found her when you were barely out of diapers."

Pauline nodded, but winced when a needle of pain stabbed through her head.

"And then you sent us to the brothel to hide us away because you didn't think Carlos would look for us there. It was an odd choice," she said and tried to quell the anger she felt—it only made her head throb. "I thought I would carry its taint forever."

"And for that I apologize, but the Madame was the only contact I could find with the time I had. The others I tried were frightened for themselves and their families. Please be comforted that your mother was never a prostitute. She entertained noblemen, but not in an improper way, at least not that anyone knows."

"So Miss Danahue is of noble birth?" the duchess asked. "I thought she looked familiar. I met the DeMarco family when the older son came to London for a season. Tsk, I'd have set my cap for him myself, but he only had eyes for Ila Danvers. And that's who you look like, Miss Danahue. Yes, now I see it."

"But why did he kill the other women?" Pauline asked. "That was him, wasn't it?"

Francesco closed his eyes and turned his head in shame. "Yes, he piled tragedy upon tragedy looking for you, and he killed young women he thought might be you. I cannot imagine the pain he's caused."

Pauline reached a hand toward him. "It's not your fault, Uncle."

"I should have made more efforts to find you and put you in a better position. We must all take responsibility for our mistakes." Francesco lifted his head, and his eyes were wet. "That is what honorable men do. I am glad that you will have a happier ending than your mother."

Pauline started to say something else, but Christopher's stricken expression stopped her.

"What is it?" she asked him.

"I need to discuss something with you, Pauline. Mother, Señor, would you leave us?"

"Let's give them a moment alone," his mother said, and her smile said that now she hoped Christopher would propose to

Pauline. She took the elbow proffered by Pauline's great-uncle. "You still have some explaining to do, Señor."

"I will be happy to, Your Grace."

Davidson doffed his hat with a curious look and disappeared behind the two older people.

Pauline turned to Christopher, expecting a reprisal of his proposal, but he looked everywhere but at her.

"I'm sorry," he said. "When I proposed to you earlier, it was rash."

Pauline's heart joined her stomach. "What do you mean?"

Christopher sat beside Pauline and took her hand. He'd been intending to tell her about what he'd done to Edward, but her uncle's words made his guilt impossible to ignore, especially now that they could be together.

"I don't know if I'm ready for a wife," he said, then shook his head at the panic that came to her eyes. "That came out wrong. What I mean is, I don't know if I deserve someone like you for a wife. You've been through so much, even as a child, and you deserve someone better than me."

"Oh?" She didn't say anything else, for which he was glad.

"Yes. You were willing to sacrifice yourself for me, but it's my fault that you were in danger. Edward would never have fallen for Lily Cavender had it not been for me, and you wouldn't have been tasked to watch over him. I'm glad you were, but I would never have willingly put you in harm's way." He stopped. He was supposed to be the eloquent older brother, but his words entangled him, as did his feelings. He had betrayed Edward because of his own desires, and he didn't want to deceive Pauline as to what sort of man she would marry. If she would still have him.

Pauline put a hand on his arm, and as always, her touch calmed him.

"What happened?" she asked.

He spilled the whole story to her, how he was tired of the traps the local mothers and their daughters laid for him, how he had told Lily that Edward was the duke as a joke, and how he was too embarrassed to step in and correct the situation when it went too far.

"I'm a horrible older brother. I acted in a completely selfish way, and both you and Edward deserve better."

"Yes, you were selfish and inconsiderate," she said. Hearing it from her lips made him feel worse.

"Can you forgive me?"

"You'll have to ask Edward. I can't forgive you for him, but I will say I don't hold you responsible for what happened here tonight. Carlos would have caught up to me eventually. And I know you would have protected me if I'd let you."

"I would have given my life for you." He kissed her hand. "And I would have died if he had killed you."

"But he didn't."

"No, he didn't." He pulled her close to him, but gently so he wouldn't injure her further.

Pauline twined her fingers in his hair. "You know what you need right now?"

"What?"

She pulled his head toward hers and whispered against his lips, "This." She kissed him, and something about her touch, her softness, her fresh scent enhanced by her time among the flowers, gave him absolution. He would talk to Edward, but to know she forgave him was enough for now.

When they broke apart, he asked, "You mean you don't hate me for betraying Edward?"

"Not at all. You've done all you could to make up for it, and you even tried to save me to save him, at the potential cost of your own life. No, you're a good big brother, and you'll make a fine husband."

"For you?" he asked.

"For me."

He took her into his arms again, but before he kissed her, he asked, "How do you always know what I need?"

"It's a gift."

Christopher took the shovel and scooped the first clod of dirt into the grave. It smelled of spring and the promise of growing things and new life, not of death. He handed the shovel back to the gravedigger, who gave it to Edward. Christopher turned, wiping the tears from his eyes. He instinctively looked around for Pauline but remembered that she wasn't there. She was at home, abed, just having given birth to their first child, a little girl.

Francesco, Pauline's great uncle, took Christopher's hand. "She was a great lady."

"Yes, she was."

Francesco didn't say anything, but the sorrow in the other man's eyes told the story, why the duchess had held on longer than anyone expected. Others said it was so she could witness the birth of her first grandchild, but Christopher suspected Francesco had something to do with it, too. He was glad she'd had the undivided love and attention of a kind man in her final days. She deserved at least that much.

Edward came to stand beside Christopher. "I have to get back to the University," he said. "I'm about to finish the modifications on the simplified aether isolater, and I can't disrupt my routine further." He wiped tears from his cheeks with the backs of his hands.

"Be careful, then. You can take the carriage. And wipe your face with this." Christopher gave his brother a handkerchief and hugged him. They both would deal with the grief in their own ways, him with his new family and Edward with his work.

He wondered if Edward would ever find someone who could deal with his intensity and quirkiness, but that wasn't under his control. At least Edward had forgiven Christopher for the misunderstanding with Lily Cavendar, although Christopher feared Edward would never trust a woman again.

Pauline's confinement and recent birthing of their daughter had excused them from hosting a funeral reception at the manor, but well-wishers came anyway, and Pauline managed to comfort them in the ways they needed. She'd told him what she could sense, and he had come to believe it, but he encouraged her to mind her own needs as well.

One thing everyone wanted to know was what they'd name their daughter. Rumor had it there was even a betting pool at the local pub. He and Pauline had discussed several names, but none seemed to fit. The duchess had been in favor of something fancy and Spanish—Francesco's influence, perhaps?—but they didn't feel right saddling the small child with a long name.

Finally, after everyone had gone and they sat, he in a winged chair, and she on a chaise, by the fire lit against the late spring chill, Pauline said, "I think I know what to name her."

"What?"

"Mary. After your mother."

He stood and went to peer over her shoulder at the baby, who was nursing. Pauline had refused a wet nurse. The child's brows were drawn into a frown that reminded him of Pauline, but he could also see the echo of his mother's favorite expression.

"I think that's perfect. Mary Bailey. And Ila would be a perfect middle name."

She looked up at him with tears shimmering in her eyes. "Yes." She turned back to the child. "Mary Ila Bailey. It fits her."

He kneaded the sore spot out of her shoulder, which had re-emerged, but not as badly as previously, and kissed the top of her head. "Duchess Pauline Bailey, I love you."

"I love you, too."

The kiss she gave him then made him think that they'd be making lots of babies together, and he was perfectly fine with that.

THANK you for reading Noble Secrets! Pauline and Christopher appeared briefly in Eros Element (keep reading), and at the suggestion of one of my readers, I decided I needed to tell their story, which takes place prior to the Aether Psychics books.

As you can tell, I do pay attention to reviews, and I'm not the only one. If you wouldn't mind, please consider reviewing the book at the site where you bought it. Book retailers like reviews, and the more a book has, the more likely they'll be to show it to other readers.

THANKS AGAIN, and happy reading!

WHAT ABOUT EDWARD?

Will he find true love and figure out how to stabilize aether? His story continues in Eros Element, the first full-length book in the Aether Psychics series.

An ancient energy. A daring expedition. Two misfit scientists in a race against time...

Iris McTavish always wanted to follow in her father's footsteps. But when his sudden death leaves her household on the brink of ruin, she may have to choose an unwanted marriage over her passion of archaeology. To save her house and prove her worth, she embarks on a mysterious and dangerous expedition...

Edward Bailey's strict scientific code holds back his anxiety and heartbreak. With his professorship and his department in danger, however, he realizes he'll need to find the secret to turning unstable aether into limitless power to keep himself afloat. And for once, Edward can't do it alone...

As Iris and Edward seek out hidden clues, they're hunted by

clockwork spies and a shadowy society. During their dash across Europe, the misfit explorers must work together to crack a worldwide energy crisis and discover the truth if they want to stay alive.

Eros Element is the thrilling first book in Aether Psychics, a series of Victorian-era steampunk adventures. If you like puzzling mysteries, incredible inventions, and a touch of magic, then you'll love Cecilia Dominic's high-spirited series.

Buy *Eros Element* today to embark on a charming clockwork adventure!

If you prefer paperbacks, you can find it online or ask your favorite physical bookstore to order it for you. To make it easy for them, you can give them the ISBN: 978-1-945074-36-3

EROS ELEMENT PREVIEW

range House, 10 June 1870
On the day of the journey, Iris woke to a very quiet house and the sense something had gone terribly wrong. Concern she'd forgotten something important had disturbed her sleep throughout the night until exhaustion claimed her. But a different kind of anxiety had awoken her this time. With a sigh, she rolled out of bed to check everything one more time.

In the dim room, she touched her trunk, valise and reticule in turn, then moved toward her maid Sophie's luggage. Instead of leather-covered wood, air met Iris's questing hand, and she hurriedly lit a lamp to reveal that Sophie's trunk was gone. She ran into Sophie's room, a small bedroom off Iris's, and found it to be empty of Sophie and all of her things. Iris's sleep-fogged mind told her Sophie had been taken by whatever had made the strange symbol on the office window.

"Sophie?" Iris called. "Sophie, where are you?"

She dashed down the stairs and found Cook in the kitchen. Her eyes were red from crying.

"Cook, where is Sophie? She's been kidnapped with all her

things." As she said it, Iris knew how silly it sounded, and her brain put together Sophie's strange absences and distant looks of the past weeks.

"Yes, Miss, but not in the way you think." Cook gestured to a letter on the table. Iris picked up the folded sheet of vellum with trembling fingers and sensed regret and fear but also joy and excitement.

The emotions must be intense for a material as flimsy as paper to hold them.

Dear Miss Iris,

I am sorry to leave you like this, but I can't bear to go on a journey. I've been seeing the Scotts' footman and was hoping you'd accept Lord Jeremy's suit so we could be together, but since you're determined to go on your adventure rather than being sensible and marrying him, I had to take matters into my own hands. With Lord Jeremy's help, we've run off to Scotland to be married. I will see you when you return and would be happy to resume my position as your lady's maid.

Best, Sophie

Accept her back after she's run off like that? Hardly. Cheeky wench! Iris's cheeks burned, and she crumpled the vellum. What was she going to do now? She couldn't go on the journey without her maid, her chaperon. What would become of her reputation?

"Miss, begging your pardon for bothering you at such a time because I know how much Miss Sophie meant to you, and I'll miss her too," Cook said. "But I need to buy eggs today since our chickens aren't laying, and I need money for the market."

"Of course," Iris said, the reality of her situation crashing down around her. "The hens seem to know when something is amiss."

"Yes, Miss. Are you still going on your journey?" Cook shot her a concerned glance, but unlike Sophie had never voiced her opinion of Iris's actions.

"I need a moment to think."

Iris went into the office, where she fetched the key for her late father's strongbox, and she opened it and counted the money remaining. Even if they were down to a household of two—and Iris would need another maid if she were to maintain the appearance of her social class—she needed to bring in an income. She closed her eyes and thought about her options—stay and accept Lord Jeremy's offer of marriage or go on the journey by herself. The thought of his shocked look when she turned him down and the idea of looking across the breakfast table at him every morning made her stomach turn. But he wanted more than just Iris... Thinking about how he would desecrate her father's study and steal his work made up her mind.

I cannot marry him. The thought asserted itself with unarguable certainty. *There's no other option. I'll go on the journey unchaperoned. If I return with my reputation ruined, it will be with enough income that Cook and I can go somewhere and start over. And if I don't return...*

She refused to consider the possibility.

A line from Sophie's letter came to mind—*with Lord Scott's help.* What if the maid had revealed the plan for the journey to her lover's employer?

The grind of wheels on the stones outside made up her mind. Iris grabbed enough money for two months of household expenses for Cook, some for herself for the journey—in case of emergencies—and slam the lid of the box. She locked it, hid it and the key and ran into the kitchen. Three loud booms echoed through the house, but Iris couldn't tell whether it was the front or side door.

"Cook, go to the door and see who it is," she called. "If it is Lord Scott, please tell him I am not at home. If it is a porter for my trunk, send him in."

"Yes, Miss."

Iris dashed upstairs and finished her toilette. She attempted to pin her hair up and hoped her buttons in the back weren't askew, but there was little she could do about either. Her fingers trembled too much.

Cook appeared in the doorway followed by a tall young man whose eyes took in everything about the bedroom including Iris herself. The look he gave her made her stand straighter and lift her chin to show she wouldn't be intimidated. Instead of bowing or looking away, his lips peeled back into the sort of smile one expected to see on the patron of a naughty peep show.

"These your things, Miss?" he asked, his tone respectful unlike his expression.

"Y-yes," Iris said. The whole situation seemed ill put-together, so she asked, "And who are you?"

"Name's Lamar. I work for Mister Cobb. Your train's in fifteen minutes. We better get a move on."

Once again, the sound of the knocker on the front door echoed through the house. Iris went to her window, where she saw the familiar lines of the Scott coach with its matched four chestnut geldings in front of the house. *Bollocks!* She couldn't remember what the itinerary had said about who would pick her up, but Lamar seemed close enough.

"Yes, we should. Take the trunk down, and I'll meet you by the back gate. Don't argue, just do it."

He complied, again looking more amused than anything else. What did he find so funny?

She embraced Cook, who grasped her upper arms.

"Oh, right." Iris pressed the household money into her hands. "This should be enough to take care of you for a couple of months."

"I don't like the feel of this, Miss." Cook's face, which looked like it had been fashioned by a pastry chef to resemble the holiday dough-dolls children received on Christmas morning, fell in lines of concern. "You're going to go off with that strange gentleman?"

"It's either that or be forced to marry Jeremy Scott. He's lazy but clever, and I have no doubt he will trap me in a compromising situation such that I will have to wed him or suffer my reputation ruined." And doom herself to a life of misery. Regardless of what her mother had said, Iris couldn't consign herself to that fate. Not without a fight.

She pecked Cook on the cheek, grabbed her reticule, traveling hat, and valise, and rushed down the stairs. "Wait five minutes and then answer the door!" she called over her shoulder. "Stall them so they won't follow me. If he catches me, he'll make me miss the train."

"Yes, Miss." Cook huffed down the stairs behind her. "I've fresh scones. That's always good for stopping a man."

Especially that one. Iris smiled, rushed through the kitchen, and into the garden. Her trunk was loaded onto an open carriage, where Lamar sat behind... Not horses, but a long cylinder that puffed out plumes of white steam.

"An open steamcoach," Iris sighed. She would have been more excited—only the wealthiest had smaller vehicles good for racing as well as driving, and she hadn't had the chance to ride in one—but she wasn't sure it could outrun the Scott team. No matter, it was better than waiting to face her doom. She tossed her valise and reticule onto the seat and climbed in before the driver could get down to hand her up. He handed back a set of goggles instead. She tried to tie her hat on while he drove away but found herself having to hold on to the side of the carriage for balance with one hand and grabbing her things with the other.

"Can you take it easier?" she asked. "I'm about to lose everything."

A whinny behind her told her that they had been spotted.

"On the other hand, hurry," she said.

"Doing the best I can, Miss. The train in front of us is more important to me than the coach behind us." He shot her a look of mixed amusement and irritation. "You were supposed to be the easy one to fetch. Those gentlemen have no idea what they're getting into with you, do they?"

Iris spared another glance behind her, where she swore the Scott coach was catching up with them. How far away was the train station? She'd often gone with her mother and the footman when they had one to drop her father off before his expeditions, but this man was taking a different route. A hard bump made her lose her grip and bang her elbow when she grabbed again for the side.

"Careful," she hissed around the pain that radiated to her collarbone. She got a hold on the carriage door handle, her fingers tingling. "Do you know where you're going?"

"I'm taking the smaller streets a steamcoach can manage better than a coach and four," he said. "Don't worry, they're falling behind."

Iris looked behind her, but a sharp pain in her neck made her have to take his word for it. After what seemed to be hours when they alternated evading their pursuers and seeming to almost fall into their clutches, the bulk of the train station rose in front of them, the train itself there. It huffed and hissed, and Iris hoped it was settling in after stopping, not getting ready to depart without her.

∽

Two days earlier…

Aetherics Department, Huntington University, England, 08 June 1870

Of all the things about the college Edward Bailey liked, the ivy was his favorite. It clung to the buildings, climbing up their stone faces, sending leafy tendrils along window edges as if peering in on lectures. On foggy days, it served as a green veil over the facades and provided a sense of decorum and discretion. He much preferred its jaunty green leaves and steadfastness through all seasons to the flashy color and riot of spring flowers with their pretty lies and false promises.

On this Monday morning, Edward tipped his hat to one particularly long tendril that hung over the door of his department building. He then ascended the cozy stairwell with its wooden rail smoothed to softness by generations of eager, curious students and gave a nod to the three discolored splotches that stood guard around the window in his office. He'd nicknamed them Hickory, Dickory and Doc due to their shapes. A fanciful notion, to be sure, but he considered them to be his guardians as he worked through the puzzles inherent in his profession.

They had not, however, prevented the department secretary, an eager young woman named Miss Ellis who eschewed sensible spectacles for a frivolously fashionable pince-nez, from putting a note on his desk about a meeting he'd neither scheduled nor desired. It was to happen in the department conference room at ten o'clock that morning, which would disrupt his routine abominably and abdominally because he timed his taking of tea such that it would provide a needed urge for a mid-morning break right around ten. Now he would have to make his tea a half hour earlier so he wouldn't end up squirming during the meeting with his chairman and his dean. They'd given him enough to squirm about in the eight years he'd been at the University.

"Well, this is most unacceptable," he muttered before his door opened to reveal the tall blond figure of Johann Bledsoe.

"Usually people talk about my unacceptability after I leave, not before I arrive," Johann said. He sat without being invited and crossed one ankle over his knee.

Politeness kept Edward from saying what he really thought about yet another interruption to his routine—goodness, what was next, a surprise visit from the queen?—but he did give his friend an exasperated look. It was quite rude of him to come in and sit without being invited.

"And to what do I owe the pleasure of this visit?" he asked, although his tone conveyed it was, indeed, not a pleasure.

"I got a note saying there would be a meeting here at ten that required my attendance. Knowing your habits, I took the liberty of coming early and having Miss Ellis make your morning tea so you wouldn't experience any awkward moments while speaking with your supervisors."

Edward's gut simultaneously twisted at the thought of having to leave the meeting to attend to bodily needs and the horror that his friend knew his habits so intimately he could plot to interrupt and adjust them to the whims of others. Underneath, he had a premonition the meeting would be the start of a life-wide disruption, perhaps an upheaval. It was time to put a stop to this nonsense.

"While I appreciate your consideration, Johann, I will not allow a meeting I neither called nor desired to interrupt this morning's important work or make a shambles of my carefully orchestrated routine, which has been developed through years of study and experimentation for maximum productivity."

"Too late, old boy. Here's Miss Ellis with your tea, twenty-three minutes early. That should give your stomach time to process it before the chair and dean arrive."

Indeed, Miss Ellis walked in carrying a tray with Edward's favorite teapot, cup and saucer set along with a half cube of sugar—she had instructions as to how he liked them split—and two teaspoons of cream in a little pitcher that had been warmed to exactly one hundred and forty degrees. Alongside were two small lemon strawberry scones, their tart fragrance mingling with that of the strong black tea to make for a siren song of scent. Brilliant, now his mind was so confused it mixed up its analogies. He'd never get anything done now.

"Your tea, Professor Bailey."

Edward put his head in his hands. Was everyone conspiring against him? His stomach growled at the aroma, and he glared toward his abdomen. He'd eaten breakfast at the normal time—why did these savage impulses betray him?

"Look at the poor gentleman," Johann said. "He's overcome with sentiment at how well we care for him."

"He's overcome with something all right, sir," Miss Ellis said, a flirtatious edge to her tone. Johann tended to do that to the fairer sex. As for his insouciant secretary, Edward didn't have the heart to reprimand her. Indeed, its caged animal beating—tea twenty-one minutes early—warred with his growling stomach.

"It's okay to emerge from your shell. She's gone. I'll pour the tea."

Edward peeked through his fingers. Johann poured two cups.

"You put the cream in first, right?"

"I've known you for how long? Yes, I fixed it the way you like it." He passed Edward the fixed tea, and Edward almost dropped the saucer on his desk, his fingers trembling.

"Thank you." He would not allow this disruption to turn him into an impolite savage, after all. "What are you doing here? If the meeting is with my chair and dean, what use could a musician be to them?"

"Perhaps they want to talk of a collaboration between our departments?"

Edward stared open-mouthed at his friend. "A collaboration? With musicians? What is this University coming to? I'm a serious scientist."

"Studying something no one seems to understand but you, and that barely."

"I am an accomplished aetherist in my field." Edward drew himself up and gestured to the stack of journals on his desk. "I have articles in all of these volumes."

"As you remind me every time I visit," Johann remarked. He set his teacup on top of the stack.

Edward drew in a gasp. "Move that at once! What if you spill?"

"Then you'll make another pile from among the dozens of spare journals you keep in your closet over there. Now tell me, how are the Duke, Duchess and ducklings? How many do they have now?"

Edward sighed. He knew Johann tried to educate him in social niceties like inquiring about family—his friend had two siblings and two parents, but Edward didn't see the point in asking about them since he never spoke with them outside of mandatory holiday gatherings—and bit his tongue so he wouldn't snap that they were irrelevant to the destruction of his morning.

He filled Johann in on what he knew of the family, but he couldn't focus. When his chair had a chance to inflict an interdisciplinary project on him, trying to stop him would be like keeping an airship from lifting once the gases were heated —it would take more than his measly efforts. Edward hoped that, like an airship, this disruption would float away and disappear, preferably before lunch.

~

Department of Archaeology, Huntington University, 08

June 1870

"Perhaps it's time for you to settle down, Miss."

Iris McTavish wrenched her mind into the present and away from the fascinating story the file in her hand told her, of frustration with academic strictures and lack of collaboration. "Not you too, Sophie." She shook her right hand, which one of her dear departed father's files had graced with a paper cut, and stuck her newly lacerated thumb in her mouth.

"I know it's not my place, Miss, but without your father bringing home his salary, how are you going to keep up the household? Cook and I are worried."

Iris rubbed her eyebrows before remembering the dust on her hands. Now she was sure she sported smudges to make her look like a stage actor or some sort of urchin. "I'm working on that."

A knock on the door forestalled the rest of the conversation, thank goodness. Sophie opened the door to reveal a messenger boy.

"Cor," he said and took off his hat with an admiring look at Sophie. "They din't tell me Professor McTavish were a ghel."

Iris stood and drew the urchin's gaze to herself. "Professor McTavish isn't—" The words stung her throat with waspish ferocity, and all she could choke out was, "available." She swallowed the sensation that tried to erupt through her chest and make her burst into tears like a schoolgirl with a broken heart. Yes, her heart was broken, but she couldn't afford silly displays of emotion.

"Oh, well, are you his secretary? Ent no one at the front desk."

"That's because it's summer," Iris's grief burst through as irritable words. "Most of the faculty are off on trips, and the department secretary's mother is ill, so she's gone to care for her." Which worked out well for Iris. Otherwise, the secretary would have breathed down her neck while she cleaned out her father's office. *She never had much use for me.*

"So who're you, Miss? Meaning no disrespect, but I got this urgent message to deliver to Professor McTavish, and if I don't, I won't get paid and we won't eat."

His voice cracked on the last word, and a tendril of tenderness curled in Iris's heart. The poor boy sounded as desperate and panicked as she felt.

"I'll take it," she said.

"How do I know you'll get it to him? My instructions were to give it to him or his assistant."

"Well, then you're in luck. I'm his assistant." Iris ignored the look Sophie shot at her and put on her gloves before she took the message from the boy. "Here's a halfpence for your trouble."

He didn't hide the disappointed look on his face, but he bobbed his head and disappeared.

"Miss..." Sophie said.

"Sometimes the universe drops things in your lap that you don't recognize as gifts at first," Iris told her. "That's what Father always said." She unfolded the slip of paper and read it, then looked at it again slowly, word by word. It was in English, and the words familiar, but the meaning didn't hit her brain until she read it out loud:

Dear Professor McTavish,

Word of your illness has reached us, and we are saddened to hear of your sudden incapacitation. However, we have a project which you will likely find interesting. If you are well enough, we have funding for you and an assistant to undertake a multidisciplinary summer expedition in search of a treasure, the likes of which has never been found. Please join us for a meeting in the Aetherics Department this Monday June 6 in the conference room on the fourth floor at ten o'clock a.m. You will be well-compensated for your time and trouble with bonus once the treasure is located and delivered.

Sincerely, Dean Hartford

College of Sciences

"It's for your father, Miss," Sophie said. "Not for you. Too bad, it would have been a good opportunity."

"It still might be. What if we tell them that my father is too ill to travel, but I'm his assistant and would be willing to undertake his duties instead?"

Sophie's mouth disappeared into a disapproving line. It reminded Iris of her mother, who would make the same expression whenever Iris would accost her father when he came home to ask about what he'd found on his expeditions, and had he brought anything for her. She later discovered the true reason for her mother's frown, but she pushed those thoughts to the back of her mind as irrelevant.

"But you're not a trained archaeologist, Miss."

"I would be if the University recognized the apprentice system, which was good enough until administrators got hold of academia. Besides, if I acquit myself well on this journey, the University may accept me as an archeology student in the fall. Then I could get a scholarship, which would help support the household beyond the money we'd get for our duties. It sounds like we'll get paid even if we don't find this treasure."

"And what if they find out your father has died?"

Iris patted her hidden skirt pocket, where she held the telegram from France. He'd gone there to see if the warmer climate would help his lungs and passed away at a sanitarium on the coast. She shared it with his chairman before he left for Bulgaria to research the symbolism of the bull in ancient European pottery, and from the department secretary's reaction when she'd shown up the previous week, she was sure the chair hadn't shared the sad news with anyone before he left, likely to keep the fallout from delaying his trip. Everyone knew he had a Bulgarian mistress. The note from the dean confirmed her secret was safe.

Had the death of Professor Irvin McTavish happened a week earlier, Iris wouldn't have been able to work the deception. But now...

"I doubt they will. Circumstances have aligned in our favor." Her shoulders hunched around the guilt sprouting in her chest at having to lie, but what else could she do? If she continued with things as they were, she and her servants would be turned out of their house in the dead of winter, or at the latest in the heat of the following summer if she could manage to sell her father's most precious artifacts. Now determination replaced guilt.

"Get ready, Sophie. You're about to become the assistant to Miss McTavish, assistant archaeologist."

Now Sophie's plump lips hopped to one side. "All right, Miss, but only because I know we need to do this. But if we're discovered, you're on your own with the punishment."

"I will do my best to protect you should that unlikely event happen." Iris moved to wipe her hands on her skirt, then stopped and looked at her gloved fingers. "Would you mind bringing me some water to wash with? We have a meeting to attend."

THANK you for reading the excerpt! You can find out more about Eros Element – including reviews and another excerpt – at http://www.ceciliadominic.com/steampunk-series/eros-element/

If you prefer paperbacks, you can also find it online or ask your favorite physical bookstore to order it for you. To make it easy for them, you can give them the ISBN: 978-1-945074-36-3

ABOUT THE AUTHOR

USA Today best-selling author Cecilia Dominic wrote her first story when she was two years old and has always had a much more interesting life inside her head than outside of it. She became a clinical psychologist because she's fascinated by people and their stories, but she couldn't stop writing fiction. The first draft of her dissertation, while not fiction, was still criticized by her major professor for being written in too entertaining a style. She made it through graduate school and got her PhD, started her own practice, and by day, she helps people cure their insomnia without using medication. By night, she blogs about wine and writes fiction she hopes will keep her readers turning the pages all night. Yes, she recognizes the conflict of interest between her two careers, so she writes and blogs under a pen name. She lives in Atlanta, Georgia with one husband and two cats, which, she's been told, is a good number of each. She also enjoys putting her psychological expertise to good use helping other authors through her Characters on the Couch blog post series.

You can find her at:

Web page: www.ceciliadominic.com

Newsletter: https://www.subscribepage.com/CeciliaDominicbackofbook

Facebook: http://www.facebook.com/CeciliaDominicAuthor

Twitter: http://twitter.com/ceciliadominic

Goodreads: https://www.goodreads.com/author/show/5011217.Cecilia_Dominic

Instagram: https://instagram.com/randomoenophile/

Cecilia's books available everywhere e-books are sold. You can also order paperback copies from Ingram Spark through your favorite physical bookstore.